Sarah's Secret

๗

Book 2

in *The Ally O'Connor Adventures*

Other books in the Ally O'Connor Adventures series:

Book 1   *Tracks in the Sand*

Other books for youth by Mark Littleton:

Aliens Among Us

God Is!

The Book of the Bible

Light the Torch, Pass the Flame: Lessons from Our Fathers

What's in the Bible for . . . Teens

Kids' Book of Devotions

The Abominable Snowbeast, part of the Get a Clue Mysteries Puzzles series

Football, part of the Sports Heroes series

Summer Olympics, part of the Sports Heroes series

Soccer, part of the Sports Heroes series

Baseball, part of the Sports Heroes series

Baseball 2: The Lives of Christian Baseball Players, from Tim Salmon to Jody Reed, part of the Sports Heroes series

Mysterious Mansion

Phantom Custodian

Cool Characters with Sweaty Palms

The Secret of Moonlight Mountain, Book 1 in the Crista Chronicles series

Winter Thunder, Book 2 in the Crista Chronicles series

Robbers on Rock Road, Book 3 in the Crista Chronicles series

Escape of the Grizzly, Book 4 in the Crista Chronicles series

Danger on Midnight Trail, Book 5 in the Crista Chronicles series

Sarah's Secret

Mark Littleton

Baker Books

A Division of Baker Book House Co
Grand Rapids, Michigan 49516

Published by Baker Books
a division of Baker Book House Company
P.O. Box 6287, Grand Rapids, MI 49516-6287

Printed in the United States of America

Library of Congress Cataloging-in-Publication Data

Littleton, Mark R., 1950–
    Sarah's secret / Mark Littleton.
       p.   cm.—(Ally O'Connor adventures ; Book 2)
    Summary: Ally and her friends, who like to think of themselves as spiritual warriors, try to help a new Korean American girl whose father is abusive.
    ISBN 0-8010-4489-8
    [1. Child abuse—Fiction. 2. Korean Americans—Fiction. 3. Christian life—Fiction.] I. Title. II. Series.
PZ7.L7364 Sar 2001
[Fic]—dc21   2001037774

For current information about all releases from Baker Book House, visit our web site:
                    http://www.bakerbooks.com

Contents

Cast of Characters

Ally O' Connor: A fun-spirited, fourteen-year-old eighth grader with a zest for life and a love for horses.

Mr. O'Connor: Ally's father, a tall, lean man with bright green eyes and a walrus-like mustache.

Mrs. O'Connor: Ally's mom, who has the same blue eyes and auburn hair as her daughter.

Nick Parker: Ally's tall, strawberry blond, teasing friend, also fourteen and an eighth grader, who has an obvious crush on Ally.

Molly Parker: Nick's earnest little sister, an eleven-year-old blond with freckles and a pure heart.

Mr. and Mrs. Parker: The fun-spirited parents of Nick and Molly.

John Debarks: A smart, sarcastic twelve-year-old with light red hair who wants to be a Pulitzer Prize winning photographer.

Kelly Debarks: A precocious ten-year-old with a mop of flaming red hair. Appears in Book 1, *Tracks in the Sand*, but not Book 2, *Sarah's Secret*.

Mr. and Mrs. Debarks: Parents of John and Kelly.

Mr. Tomoro: A naturalized American citizen of Japanese descent who speaks with the accent of his parents; a widower and beloved neighborhood storyteller, who houses the largest shark tooth collection in the Outer Banks.

Dunk: Mr. Tomoro's playful and beloved black labrador. Is seen in Book 1, *Tracks in the Sand*, but not in Book 2, *Sarah's Secret*.

Sarah Matthews: The new kid in Ally and Nick's school, Sarah is a meek and quiet girl, Asian in appearance and descent (her mother is Korean). She is also a talented gymnast.

Mr. Matthews: Sarah's father.

Mrs. Matthews: Sarah's mother.

Colonel: Mr. Matthews's big, beautiful, brown, thoroughbred horse.

Willie: Mr. Matthews's dog.

Coach James: The gymnastics coach at school.

Mr. Bellows: The janitor at the school/gym.

One

The Haunted House

"It's so quiet here," said Ally O'Connor as she peered over three-foot-high cornstalks to a farmhouse beyond. A breeze blew her auburn bangs into her eyes. She brushed them back.

"They say it's haunted," Nick replied. He was Ally's neighbor and best friend. Both fourteen, they went to the same school and had spent family summer vacations together as far back as they could remember.

"Then who planted all this corn?" Ally asked, rolling her eyes. "Ghosts?"

"Ghost corn-planters," Nick said solemnly, poking his little sister, Molly, in the ribs. Nick and Molly, both blond and tanned from summer, were look-alikes except Molly was shorter.

Ally laughed at Nick's joke, but Molly didn't move. "I don't think we should go farther," she said.

Nick shrugged. "Come on, let's go to the pond at least. It's not on the farm property, and I've heard the town is going to make a park out there. It'll be cool!"

"Do you mean cool as in chilly?" Ally asked. "Or do you mean cool as in fun, exciting, different, noteworthy?"

Nick glanced at Ally and then Molly. "Who is this, the dictionary lady?"

"Don't ask me. You're always bringing her along," Molly said, laughing.

Ally grinned and gave Nick a little kick. "Go then, but if you fall into that scummy pond, don't blame anyone but yourself."

Nick stepped onto a path at the edge of the cornfield and moved forward as if he owned the whole country-side. Ally gave Molly a "should-we-or-shouldn't-we?" look.

Molly nodded, then said, "If we die, I'm blaming Nick."

"That's okay," Ally said, nodding to Nick in mock sympathy. "He gets blamed for just about everything else."

The two girls caught up to Nick's pace. Cornstalks rustled against their shirts as they passed. The air smelled of dirt, dust, and the green scent of summer. To Ally it was lively and inviting, as if the field were saying, "Enjoy today. Make the most of every minute."

Within minutes they reached the pond. Stooping down to hide behind the corn rows, Nick motioned to the farmhouse on their left. "See, it looks empty."

He was right. Nothing stirred. Neat and tidy rows of corn stretched in each direction around it, but the house itself looked old and sad. It seemed abandoned in the middle of a barnyard.

At that moment Ally remembered one of her recurring nightmares. In her dream, she is standing outside a haunted house. Everything is eerily silent until a ghost suddenly reaches out and grabs her. She usually would wake up in a sweat, glance wildly around, then fix her eyes on a pile of clothes that suddenly looked dark and evil! Now, Ally's gaze was fixed on that old farmhouse. *No way,* she thought, *do I want to get closer.* She had a feeling something was wrong there, something she wanted to stay away from.

Then a better thought came into Ally's mind. "Let's walk toward the house," she said bravely, somewhat surprising herself. "Then if there are any people around, they can show themselves right off the bat." She was hoping that then she wouldn't have to be afraid and could have fun hanging out at the dam that crossed the pond without worrying about ghosts.

Ally thought Nick probably wanted to go right through the corn to the dam, where they would take any resident ghosts by surprise too. Nick, after all, was good at sneaking around.

She was right. Nick stepped onto a path leading to the pond.

"To the water and beyond," he whispered, smiling and widening his eyes. "If we die, we die together."

Ally gripped his arm. "Don't get weird on us, Nick," she said. "This place gives me the creeps."

Nick jogged forward, tripping over clumps of dirt. Ally and Molly followed until the threesome had reached the pond where sunlight didn't seem to brighten the dark water.

Nick studied the murky, deep pond.

"Might the Loch Ness monster lurk within?" he wondered out loud.

Ally could hear rushing water and turned toward the dam. It blocked the far end of the pond. On either side of a mossy concrete wall, two large disks projected from the base. For a second, Ally wasn't sure what they were. Then she realized they must be screws to open and shut the sluice where water tumbled over the edge.

"Let's go out on the dam," Nick said.

Ally had second thoughts. "Are you kidding?" she said. "It's slippery, and we'd be stranded if a ghost showed up."

"No one's coming. Look! The place is a graveyard!"

Ally glanced at Molly. "That's what I mean!"

Molly gazed at the dam. "I can beat up a ghost any day," she said. Though Molly was only eleven, sometimes she was even braver than Nick.

"Okay," Ally said, shielding her eyes from the harsh sunlight. "Let's do battle with the banshee of the cornfields."

Nick stepped out onto the dam. At four feet wide, it could be easily crossed by the threesome walking side-by-side. But the concrete was crumbly and slick with wet moss.

"Don't slip," Ally said. "You'll go over. Who knows what's swimming below, waiting with hungry eyes fixed on your legs!"

"Not mine," Nick said. "Your legs—your lovely legs!"

"Oh, thanks a lot!" Ally answered, laughing so much she almost lost her balance.

"No, really, Ally," Molly said. "You're going to be a glamorous movie star someday."

Ally shook her head. "Sorry. I'm going to be a vet."

"Cool!" Nick said gleefully. "A veteran! And in which war will you do battle?" Nick loved war stories and could turn any conversation into talking about them.

"The Nick-Needs-To-Hurry Wars!" Ally replied. "Now get going!"

"Take baby steps," Nick advised himself as much as the girls as they inched onto the dam.

When they reached the sluice, Ally heard something. "What was that?" she asked Nick and Molly.

"What?" Nick asked.

"It sounds like a cat. Or someone crying," Ally said. "It's coming from those trees!"

Suddenly a large spotted dog leapt out of the trees on the far side of the dam. With amazement, then terror, Ally,

12

Nick, and Molly watched at least ten other dogs swarm to greet them, teeth bared and growling. A man's voice rose above the barking, "What you got, boys, huh?"

As the dogs scurried toward the dam, Ally turned to run, with Molly right behind her.

Then someone screamed, "Help!" Nick skittered on the top of the dam, twisted to catch himself, but plunked into the pond.

Ally and Molly stopped to stare as Nick floundered behind them in the murky water. Two of the dogs had advanced slowly toward them. Nick looked up and saw more dogs waiting at the edge, as if to swallow him the moment he emerged from the water.

"Stay calm," Ally told Molly.

"Sure. That would make a great headline," Molly answered. "Kids Calm as Dogs Devour Them."

On shore, a man in a black hat rode into sight. He was sitting on a majestic brown thoroughbred. "What're you doin' on myyy pro-ah-perty?" he shouted, his voice slurred.

When Ally didn't answer, Nick, still treading water, asked, "Will your dogs attack?"

"If I saaay so," the man said gruffly. "Now get off myyy pro-ah-perty!"

Molly stepped forward. "Sir, we thought this pond was part of a park. We didn't know anyone lived here. We heard . . ."

"You heard wrong!" the man boomed. He moved uneasily, seeming to lose his balance in the saddle, then righted himself. "Trespassing! That's what you're doin'. Din't you see the signs?"

For the first time Ally noticed NO TRESPASSING signs posted on the trees by the dam. How had she not seen them before? "We're sorry, sir; we didn't see them," she said. "We'll be happy to go, and we'll never come back!"

Behind the man someone wandered out of the trees. "Daddy! Dad!" a small, weak voice said. An Asian girl with long, tousled hair and almond eyes came to stand beside the horse. Her face was red and puffy from crying, and her clothes were wrinkled. "Dad, please let them go," she pleaded to the big man who towered above her.

"Get!" the man growled, then shouted, "Get home to your mama, girl!"

The girl ran into the house, slamming the screen door with a whap.

"You came sneaking around here to steal!" he shouted back at Nick, Ally, and Molly.

"We didn't!" Nick hollered from the pond. "We just thought the dam was cool."

"Cool?" The man squinted.

Just then a woman ran out of the farmhouse, yelling in another language. *Japanese,* Nick thought, *like Mr. Tomoro at the Outer Banks where we vacation.*

"Get back in there!" the man said to the woman.

She backed away toward the house, but shook her fist at the man on the horse.

The man swiveled in the saddle as if he might slip off, then regaining his grip, turned to Ally, Molly, and Nick. "I told you to get off my property and don't come back," he rasped. When he slapped his thigh, the dogs raced around the edge of the pond back to his feet dangling at the sides of the tall horse.

"Never come back, you hear?" the man yelled as he wheeled the horse around and galloped into the old barn. "Willie!" he whistled, then yelled, "You go, boy!"

Willie, the largest of the dogs, hurried back to wait at the edge of the pond as Ally and Molly stepped off the dam on the other side. Nick clambered out of the water, his feet sinking into the mud. The threesome hurried into the corn rows with Willie following about ten feet back. He growled as they paused. Reaching the road, the dog stopped, barked, then turned and bounded back through the corn to the farm.

14

"I'll be glad never to go back there," Nick said with a quiver in his voice. He was soaking wet and caked with mud.

"We're lucky we weren't mauled," Ally said. "But who was that girl? I don't remember ever seeing her before."

"Yeah," Nick said, "and I bet we'll never see her again."

Ally stared back down the road toward the farm. She wondered what it must be like to have a father who yelled, was mean, and hated anyone new.

A New Gymnastics Star

"Wow, look at that girl go," Ally said with a whistle the next day at gymnastics practice. From the looks of it, the summer gymnastics team had a new star. This girl had finesse, strength, and fluid grace. Ally had never seen a gymnast this good in real life. Then Ally gasped—not just at the girl's talent, but at the obvious pain she witnessed as the new gymnast seemed to favor her left side.

No, it was something else and the last thing she expected: The Asian girl from the farmhouse! Today this girl looked pretty in her leotard and with her straight hair combed into a gleaming rope that hung down her back. She was working out on the uneven parallel bars, where Nick and Molly stood gaping at her high-flying stunts.

"Are you sure it's the girl from the farm?" Ally asked Molly.

Molly nodded. "I saw her drive up with her mom. It's the same person. Coach James seemed to be expecting them."

"I wonder what she's doing here," Ally said. "And where did she come from?"

Just then, the girl performed a difficult maneuver, then hung upside down with her legs crimped over the wooden bar. A second later, she flipped down, landing on her feet. As she struck the ground, she suddenly grabbed her side and winced, giving a sign of pain. Ally was worried. What was wrong?

"I wonder what her name is," Molly said, brushing a strand of sun-bleached hair out of her mouth.

"I don't know," Ally said. "Maybe they just moved onto the farm."

As Nick leaped onto the side horse and scissored his legs, the coach shouted, "Right on!" Nick hopped off and waved to Ally and Molly.

"Come on," Ally waved back. "Let's talk to that girl."

The three friends crossed the room, and Nick combed one hand through his hair. It always made Ally laugh the way he preened when a pretty girl happened to be around. Was this new girl going to be her rival this summer? Ally smiled at the thought. Nick was so obvious about everything. Maybe that was his charm, though, the fact that he never lied. Ally liked knowing that with Nick, what you saw was what you got.

As they approached, the new girl did a quick kip up onto the bars. Nick leaned against the poles supporting them. "You're good," he said boldly.

The girl looked down. She gave no indication that she recognized Nick. She pitched herself over the bar, swinging, but didn't make the complete 360-degree arc. Dismounting with a back flip, she nailed it with a sharp whap. But a second later she once again grabbed her side. Ally looked for Coach James, but he was on the other side of the room.

"Are you okay?" Ally asked, stepping toward the girl.

"Yes, of course," she said, turning away.

"Shouldn't you have a spotter?" Nick asked. He was referring to a person who would watch and catch her if she slipped.

"Mr. James hasn't mentioned it yet," the girl murmured.

"What's your name? Are you from the farm out east?" Ally asked.

Suddenly the girl's face flushed with shame. "I'm sorry," she said quickly. "I didn't recognize you."

Ally blushed too. "So you were at the pond?"

"My name is Sarah Matthews. I'm sorry about my father," she said, looking down.

"No big deal," Nick replied. "I can spot you," he added, glancing at Ally and Molly. "Have you been doing this long?"

"Since I can remember," Sarah said. "It's the only thing that keeps me. . . ." She broke off the thought by looking away. "Keeps me in shape," she whispered, turning back to Ally and shaking back her long black ponytail.

Sarah started to hold out her hand. Nick returned it with a polite handshake of his own.

"Are you Japanese?" Nick asked.

Ally gave Nick an annoyed look for being so rude, then quietly studied Sarah's face. Her eyes were dark, shadowed by finely sculpted eyebrows and delicate cheekbones. Her olive skin was soft and clear.

"No. My mother is Korean," Sarah said. She stopped, then turned away again.

"Why did you move here?" Ally asked.

Sarah said haltingly, "My father's American. He met Mother when he was in South Korea with the army."

Nick nodded with understanding. "Did you live in Seoul?"

"No, a smaller town farther north where there was an American military base."

Sarah looked up at the bars. "I learned gymnastics there at a Korean school. I was going to be on the Korean team," she said. "Then my father was transferred back to the United States. He later bought the farm. My mother wants

18

me to continue to practice. Maybe I can't be on a big national team, but I still like to scissor and swing." Sarah grabbed hold of the bars above her.

"I'm trying to learn something new," Sarah said. "I'm sure Mr. James will give me spotters later."

"Oh, we can do it," Ally said. "He won't mind."

"Are you sure?" Sarah's hesitation made Ally wonder if she was afraid.

"He won't mind, I'm sure," Ally said. "But he wouldn't like you trying something new without using spotters."

Sarah's eyes went wide, and she hung her head. "I did something wrong." She jumped down from the bars.

As Sarah stepped off the mat, Ally touched her arm. "It's okay. You didn't know. Go ahead. Mr. James won't be mad at you."

"Are you sure?"

"Yes."

Ally said, "I'll get on the other side. You get in the back, Molly."

Sarah glanced at Ally with worry, then grabbed the bar, kicking her legs out to swing. She wore square patches of terrycloth on her palms. They were laced into her fingers and strapped around her wrists to protect them. Other members of the team gathered around now to watch. One of the team members dragged another rubber mat under the bars to cushion Sarah's landing.

Sarah swung under the top bar, splitting her legs to scoot over the lower bar and then cocking her body to build momentum. Her hands gripped the bar so tightly they looked white. Everyone began cheering, arousing Coach James's attention. Quickly he came running over.

"Hey!" he shouted. "What's going on here?"

The kids stepped back to let him through. Sarah didn't seem to hear him. It was as if she had been transported to another world, a place where she could fly high above everything that happened on earth.

Sarah flung herself out into the air with abandon.

"Stop this!" Mr. James shouted. "I thought I told you. . . ."

Sarah kept going. Ally saw her take a deep breath, that faraway look still in her eyes.

Mr. James blew his whistle. Sarah went rigid and turned, her face startled as she slowed her momentum and dropped to the floor.

"I'm sorry, I thought . . . !" Sarah cried.

"What you're doing is dangerous," he answered quickly but with a gentle tone in his voice. "We don't have trained spotters. Now all of you—nobody on the uneven bars without my permission. You have to get spotters." Mr. James saw that his correction upset Sarah so he gestured to show he meant what he said for all the kids at the gym.

"We were spotting," Nick said. "She was okay."

"No back talk, Nick Parker," Mr. James said more seriously to Nick.

Sarah gave the coach an embarrassed, fearful look, then said meekly, "I'm sorry, Mr. James. I thought if I had spotters it was okay."

The coach set his whistle in his mouth and blew: Tweeeeeet! "Everyone on the mats now. Team meeting!" He glanced at Sarah, then whispered to her, "You stay here a second, Sarah."

Sarah hung her head.

Nick and Ally were reluctant to just walk away from her, but as the other gymnasts rushed by, they slipped into the group.

"Is he going to yell at her?" Molly asked. "We were going to spot. We told him that."

"Yeah, but she's not just doing skin-the-cat," Nick said.

"She's really good," Ally said, looking back at Coach James talking seriously to the slim girl. "I hope he doesn't scare her. It's her first day, for heaven's sake."

20

"We should talk to her after practice," Molly said. "We could find out more about the farm and invite her to our clubhouse. We could make her a member and everything!"

Ally nodded distractedly. She was curious about why Mr. James had singled out Sarah. He was talking more privately to her than he might to others on the team. Still, Sarah hung her head and Ally saw her eyes well up with tears. It seemed strange, because Coach James never lost his temper, and he treated everyone with respect, even when he had to correct them. He seemed especially sensitive to Sarah right now, correcting her in private. But perhaps Sarah felt she would lose the privilege of working out since she didn't play by the rules.

"Mr. James is a big old fleep!" Ally said aloud.

"A fleep?" Molly asked, giving Ally a little punch. "What's that?"

"Somewhere between a flop and a flerp!"

Both of them cracked up.

"Man, Ally," Nick said, overhearing their conversation. "You come up with some good ones."

After the team meeting, during which Sarah sat off to one side by herself, Ally grabbed Molly's shoulder. "Let's find out what happened," she said.

"Okay," Molly answered. "But Mr. James may not like us interfering."

"He won't even know," Nick interrupted. "Anyway, he always tells us it's more important to be kind than to be right. He wants us to be friendly, especially since Sarah's new. Besides, she might want to go out with me," he joked.

"Figures," Ally said.

"Hey, I can't make any headway with you," Nick said, grinning.

"Fine with me," Ally said. "Just don't breathe on her after you've eaten one of your flaming burritos."

Nick breathed mockingly in Ally's direction. She ducked.

Just then Sarah arrived at the door. Her mother was waiting in the truck at the curb.

"You okay?" Ally asked Sarah.

"I'm sorry," she said, tears in her eyes. "I'm sorry."

"Don't worry about Mr. James," Ally said, following Sarah to the street. "He's just covering his own hide to make sure no one gets hurt."

"I should have known the rules," Sarah said. "I'm sorry."

"It's okay," Nick said. "Don't worry about it."

As Ally watched Sarah get into the truck beside her mother, she noticed a reddish-blue mark just below her hairline. Was it a bruise? *How odd,* Ally thought. *I wonder where that came from?* She shrugged it off, thinking maybe it was from an injury on the bars. But something about the way Sarah had hung her head and the way she was always saying "I'm sorry" wasn't quite right. Just as Sarah pulled the door shut, Ally saw another mark on Sarah's thigh. It was a big purple bruise, too big to come from the bars.

Three

Friendship Is Born

At the next team meeting, Coach James was blabbering on and on about the teams they'd be competing with later that summer. It was hot, and Ally—who was in this more for the fun than any medals—was sweaty, tired, and distracted. She passed a note to Molly:

Molly, let's ask Sarah to walk home with us today. I think she's cool. What do you think? Ask Sarah when you have a chance. Maybe we'd better leave Nick out of it. He might breathe on her.

Ally

Molly wrote back:

I think she's cool, too. Let's invite her to the clubhouse. I survived Nick's breath, but he could use a dozen mints.

Molly

P.S. Maybe we'd better stop joking about Nick's breath. He might eat something really terrible and kill us both with it—on purpose!

When the meeting was over, Coach James officially introduced Sarah Matthews as a new member of the team. Everyone crowded round, wanting to meet the new and obvious talent. Ally poked Nick in the side when he sidled beside her.

"Girl stuff, Nick, babe," Ally said. "Make tracks."

"Aw, come on. Sheesh! Girls are nuts."

"You mean mysterious," Ally said, pushing him away. "Now go, and may the force be with you."

"Thanks a bunch, babe." Nick said, pulling a face at Ally. "I'll find my own way home."

Molly was already talking to Sarah.

"Yeah, I'd like to," Sarah replied. "But I have to call my mom first."

Molly and Sarah walked over to where Ally was helping Nick stuff all his gymnastics equipment into his sports bag.

"Nick," Ally said. "Don't go yet. Look who's coming."

"Oh, do I have your permission to stick around?"

"Yeah, just don't breathe."

"There's nothing wrong with my breath, Ally!"

"Yeah, but you never know . . . if you go hanging out at Taco Pete's."

Sarah sidled over, and Nick blushed suddenly.

"You want to see our clubhouse?" Ally asked.

Sarah looked down at her feet. "I'm supposed to go right home after practice. I have chores."

"It's just a little walk," Nick piped up, glancing at Ally. "At most, ten minutes out of your way. Max."

"You'll be close enough to get home quickly," Ally added, thinking she wouldn't want Sarah's father mad at her about anything. "But you can call if you want. I have my mom's cell phone with me."

Sarah hung her head slightly. "All right."

"Cool!" Nick said, shooting his fist in the air. "You'll love it. Guaranteed."

Sarah dialed the number.

"Mom," she said into the receiver. "I'm going to walk home, but I'll be there soon. Is Dad . . ." She glanced at Ally, Nick, and Molly uneasily. "Is Dad all right?"

Ally strained to hear what Mrs. Matthews might be saying, but the voice on the other end hummed low into a whisper.

"Okay, I'll be home by three-thirty. Thanks, Mom."

Sarah clicked off the phone. "Okay," she said, looking suddenly relieved, but still not relaxed.

Nick grinned. The foursome traipsed out of the meeting room, down the hall, and into the summer sunshine. The air smelled of newly mown grass and crab apples.

"Calm down, Super Boy," Ally whispered as they went.

"I am calm!" Nick sniped, looking annoyed.

"I can hear your heart pounding," Ally teased.

Nick kicked at the dirt. "Yeah, well, I can hear. . . ."

"What? What can you hear?"

"Your stomach gurgling."

Ally laughed. "Okay, Mr. Comedian!"

Ally took a deep breath. "Nothing like a gulp of unsweaty air after being in the gym," she announced with a flair. She sucked her breath in deeply. "I love the scent of the pines."

"Wash your hair with Pine Sol," Nick laughed. "That'll give you the scent all the time."

"Breathing deep is good for your circulation," Sarah suddenly volunteered. "My mother says it 'reoxygenates' your blood. You get out all the gunk."

It was the first time Sarah had lightened up since Coach James scolded her, and Ally was glad.

The kids hiked the hill onto Pine Woods Lane where Ally, Molly, and Nick lived on Lake Pakomee. Before long, the girls slid into a jog behind Nick. If they cut through some yards and took a path behind Ally's house, they could reach the clubhouse faster.

"So your dad was in the army?" Ally asked Sarah.

Sarah stumbled over a stone in the path. "My dad was a sergeant," she said.

"His horse was beautiful," Ally offered.

"That's Colonel," Sarah said. "My father wants to breed him and make money on racing horses."

"Do you ever ride him?"

"Oh, sure," Sarah said. "When my dad is okay with it, that is."

"Your dad seems . . . tough," Ally searched for the right words, to find out why Sarah's father had been so angry by the pond.

A dark look came over Sarah's face. "My dad is into rules," she said tensely, glancing at her watch. "In fact, I'd better hurry."

"Come on, guys," Nick said. "That ten minutes is fading fast."

Ally worried that she'd offended her new friend, because Sarah said nothing more. Just then they reached the clubhouse. Built of old barn planks nailed into a copse of trees, it rose three levels from the ground.

"Wow! You built this?" Sarah said, stepping through the doorway, smiling for the first time.

Nick showed her the ladder to the second level.

Nick showed Sarah how to climb up. In another minute, all four of them stood on the top story.

"What a view!" Sarah exclaimed.

Molly helped Nick explain how they'd built it and how much fun they'd had there. "Sometimes we use it as a Bible club, and we talk about what it means to be spiritual warriors."

Within minutes Sarah was looking at her watch. "I'd better go now," she announced.

26

Ally wondered if talking about the Bible had scared Sarah. Maybe, from living in another country, they had another religion. Ally whispered a prayer under her breath that God would let Sarah be their friend.

The kids climbed down to walk Sarah home. They were about to cross the street when a dirty pickup truck turned the corner.

Sarah gasped, "Uh-oh!"

The truck squealed to a stop.

"Sarah!" the rough-looking man shouted, leaning out through the passenger window. "You've got chores."

"I'm sorry, Dad."

Ally saw Sarah's hand shaking.

The man took the truck out of gear. "Get in!" he growled.

"Dad, I just wanted to see my friends' clubhouse."

"Get in! I've been drivin' everywhere lookin' for you!"

Ally watched as the hulking man slid across the front seat. He opened the door and stepped out. "What did I tell you to do?"

Sarah shivered. "I'm coming."

The man grabbed Sarah's arm and led her into the truck.

Ouch! Ally thought, though Sarah had fallen silent.

Her father shoved Sarah into the cab, then turned to Ally, Molly, and Nick. "If you have any sense, you won't go messing with my kid," he said between gritted teeth. "Understand?"

Ally gulped. Up close the man looked like the Incredible Hulk. *He has to be at least six-foot-five,* she thought. His punched-in nose looked like it had been broken in too many fights.

Sarah slumped in the front seat of the truck. Ally thought she heard muffled sobs.

"You hear me?" the man yelled out the window to Nick, Ally, and Molly.

"How can we not?" Nick muttered.

"Don't give me any lip, kid. I'll bust it." The man stared down at Nick, then gave Ally and Molly a quick once-over.

As he slammed the door shut, Ally heard him say to Sarah, "What's wrong with you? No dawdling till the chores are done. You know that!"

The engine roared, and a billow of smoke soared out as the truck screeched away.

Molly coughed. "How can he treat her like that?"

"That guy is nasty," Nick said when the air cleared.

"He thinks he's still in the army," Ally added.

"We'd better keep an eye on Sarah," Nick added. "Something's not right." He gazed at Ally and Molly with a deep-in-thought look. "Let's plan a party," he added, "then go visit Sarah to invite her. He won't keep her from going to a party with friends."

"Well, he thinks we're punks," Ally said, her eyes suddenly burning with anger, "but maybe we can change that sooner if not later."

Four

The Party Invitation

"How should we do this?" Ally asked no one in particular, sitting in the middle of her friends on the floor of their treehouse.

"Give Sarah and her dad about an hour," Nick said. "She should have her chores done by then. Then we can go over and scout it out. You know, like the twelve spies scouting out the Promised Land."

The girls just stared blankly at him.

"Book of Joshua. Don't you guys know that song that goes, 'Ten were bad and two were good'?"

"I know the story," Ally said. "Joshua, Caleb, and ten others spied out the Promised Land. They saw giants, and ten of the spies argued they were too big. But Caleb and Joshua bravely believed God was with them so the giants couldn't hurt them."

"So what are you saying, Nick?" asked Molly. "That God is with us among giants?"

"Of course," Nick said, as if he'd just thought of that part. He squinted slyly.

Ally felt like they were patriots discussing the plan to take America from the British. "So I'll be Joshua. Who wants to be Caleb?" she asked.

"This isn't a game, Ally," Molly suddenly said. "Sarah's father is creepy, and he's a giant."

"I wonder what he has to hide," Nick said suddenly.

"Hide?" Molly answered. She looked at Nick and at Ally. "What do you mean?" Her pretty face was dark with worry.

"All I'm saying is that he acts like a person who has something to hide," Nick said. "I didn't say I know what it is. Who knows, maybe he grows pot or something."

"Pot?!" the girls said at once.

"The drug?" Nick said. "From hemp. Some people do grow drugs on their property."

"That's awful! Wouldn't the police get him?" Ally asked.

"Not if he does it secretly," Nick said.

"Do you think Sarah would know?" Molly searched Nick's eyes anxiously.

"That may be why she's so scared all the time," Nick said.

"I think she's scared because he's mean to her," Ally said. "Did anyone notice how she was protecting her left side at practice every time she landed?"

Molly nodded. "Like she was sore."

"You don't think her dad beats her?" Nick wondered aloud.

Molly looked worried and Ally noticed. "By the way," she interrupted, "I asked my dad about the pond and it is public property. He knows that."

"So Sarah's father lied?" Molly asked.

"Well, maybe he thinks it's his," Ally answered.

Just then they heard someone walking through the trees. It was John Debarks, another neighbor, with his camera, as usual. At twelve years old, he was the unofficial club photojournalist.

"Oh, no!" cried Nick, "The neighborhood spy has come to infiltrate our defenses."

"Hey," John responded, "who was that guy anyway—the one yelling from that pickup?"

Everyone took turns telling John about Sarah and her angry dad.

"Well, let's go, then," John said with enthusiasm. "I'll take my camera, and we'll see just what kind of situation this Sarah is in. You never know when you might need photos," he added, focusing the lens on Ally.

"What about the dogs, Nick?" Ally said.

"We have to take pepper spray. My mom's got some in a drawer somewhere."

"What?" Ally, Molly, and John cried in unison.

"If the dogs come after us, we'll get them to back off with the spray."

"Unhhht!" Ally said, imitating the sound of a game show buzzer. "You think Sarah's dad is mad now. Wait till his dogs come running home and he sees someone's shot them with pepper spray. He'd come after us with an armored tank. Besides, it's not right to take something like that from your mom's drawer without asking first."

Nick frowned. "What should we do then?"

"I say something totally unexpected," Ally said.

"What?" the other three asked.

"Listen to this!" Ally said, reaching for her friends to huddle.

Mrs. Parker, Nick and Molly's mom, stood bending over sheets of cookies as the foursome stepped into her kitchen. She was a slender woman with long wavy hair who still wore her old hippie hoop earrings.

"Hey, Mom, would you take us over to a friend's house?" Molly asked as innocently as she could.

"I'm baking, honey," Mrs. Parker said.

"It'll just take a few minutes," Molly said, glancing at Ally as if looking for guidance. "We want to invite this new girl, Sarah, to a party at the clubhouse. Please . . ."

Mrs. Parker looked up, wiping beads of sweat off her forehead with a towel. "Oh, I guess I can take a break between batches. Where is it?"

"Just down the road."

"Okay," she grinned. "When these next Snicker Doodles come out of the oven, I'll shut down the production line for a while."

Soon they were bumping down the rough dirt road in the Parkers' car to the main highway. Mrs. Parker turned left and found the road to the farm a half mile farther. But a closed aluminum gate blocked their path. On the front was a large sign:

NO HUNTING

NO FISHING

NO TRESPASSING

Ally couldn't read the signature at the bottom, but she made out an "M" on the last name and assumed it was Mr. Matthews. More signs hung on the fences on either side of the gate where you couldn't miss them. Ally figured Sarah's father had hung up even more signs since they'd been playing at the dam.

Mrs. Parker turned around to look from Ally to Nick, and back. "Just who is this new friend?" she said. "And why is her father so concerned about trespassers?"

Nick cleared his throat. "He's just a farmer, Mom." He hopped out, checked the gate, and finding it was unlocked, opened it then jumped back into the car.

Mrs. Parker narrowed her eyes. "I don't like this. You kids had better not be putting me on about something." She drove through the gate and down the long driveway to the farmhouse. A dog barked. Seconds later, the whole pack roared out of the barn and surrounded the van.

"What on earth?" Mrs. Parker cried, frowning at Nick and Ally.

"They're just dogs," Molly said, rolling up her window.

"They don't look very friendly," Mrs. Parker said, clearly not liking what she saw.

As the car moved slowly forward through the dogs, John said, "Hey, look at that!"

In the middle of a patch of clover stood a tall, shuttered box. It was painted white and looked shabby.

Suddenly, Ally noticed bees everywhere. They whizzed by, buzzing like mini fighter airplanes. One flew into the crack she'd left in her window. She ducked and swung at it.

"It's a beehive," Nick said. "Sarah's dad must be cultivating honey."

"Out here?" John said.

"Yeah, why not?" Nick answered. "It would be cool to get a net suit and look inside at the hives. Look, there are others." He pointed through the orchard where several other beehives stood like a line of soldiers.

Mrs. Parker, with dogs flanking her van and barking like maniacs, pulled in front of the old farmhouse. A man stepped out from behind the screen door. Mr. Matthews looked as angry as a pit bull. His lips curled into a snarl.

Mrs. Parker rolled down her window. "Sir," she said, smiling, "we wanted to invite your daughter to a party."

"I thought I told you kids not to be messin' around with my daughter! And now you're messin' around on my property. I 'spose you saw my signs," Mr. Matthews said, eyeing Nick, Ally, Molly, and John, but ignoring Mrs. Parker. Ally saw Sarah standing behind him in the shadows. She looked frightened and worried.

"We saw a sign, yes," Mrs. Parker said, cool as chilled lemonade. "But we aren't hunting or fishing. We just want to invite Sarah over." She smiled again at the big man like he was an old friend she'd just run into. Ally knew Mrs. Parker wasn't intimidated.

"No trespassing," Mr. Matthews said curtly. His eyes squinted beneath the brim of his black derby. "I guess I have to call the police."

"Please, Daddy," Sarah said as she ran up to the car. "They didn't mean any harm."

"Maybe I oughta sic my bees on you," Mr. Matthews said to Nick's mom. He laughed as he said this, but there was a seriousness to his manner. In fact, Ally noticed, his big eyes glowered.

"We wanted to invite Sarah to a party and swimming in the lake," Molly said, sticking her head out the window behind her mother's. "We just want to be friends."

"Sarah doesn't need more friends," Mr. Matthews growled. He waved his arm at Sarah. "Now you get to the barn and finish your chores."

Ally noticed Sarah had the same look as when Coach James reprimanded her—a look of shame and fear.

"But, Dad, . . ." Sarah started to try calming him.

"Don't sass me!" Mr. Matthews swung around. Sarah instinctively stepped backwards, almost tripping over some stones. As she backed away, the man turned again to Mrs. Parker. "You just sit here."

Now Mrs. Parker tried to soothe him. "Please understand, Mr. Matthews, we just want to invite Sarah—"

"I don't like anybody sneakin' around on my land," Mr. Matthews interrupted.

Mrs. Parker laughed. "Look, no need to call the police. We'll get going right now. I'm sorry to have bothered you."

The nasty look in Mr. Matthews's eyes didn't change, but he suddenly laughed. "You think I don't have my rights?"

"Of course," Mrs. Parker said. "But I don't think the sheriff needs to be concerned with this. Don't you think he has real criminals to catch?"

"You wait right here," Mr. Matthews said and turned to stomp back into the farmhouse.

"I think we'll just be going," Mrs. Parker said. She rammed the van into gear, backed up a bit, then turned the wheel and burst forward.

The last thing Ally saw was Mr. Matthews's dogs swirling around each other after the car pulled away.

Mrs. Parker drove home in silence, mulling over what just happened. Ally sensed her distress and leaned forward.

"Now you know why we had to go over there," Ally said. "We had to see what Sarah was up against."

Mrs. Parker nodded. "I don't know what to tell you, kids. That man clearly has problems. But you're not the ones to handle them." She was stern, looking at Nick, then glancing quickly over her shoulder to say with her eyes, "I mean it."

"But he could hurt Sarah, if he hasn't already," Ally said. "I think she needs our help." Ally looked to the others who all nodded.

"I hear you, honey," Mrs. Parker said. "But I think there's not much we can do except sit tight."

She turned onto the dirt road, pulled into her driveway, and stopped to look closer at everyone. "Maybe we should pray for Sarah."

"Pray?" Nick said.

"That's what Christians do," Mrs. Parker smiled. "God can help us know what to do. You say that Sarah's in your gymnastics group? I think I'll call Coach James, too."

"About what?"

"To be watching out for her. Who knows what her father's like."

"Let's pray for her right now," Ally said.

Mrs. Parker asked God to protect Sarah and help her family. But as Ally got out of the van, her heart felt heavy. She sensed Sarah needed the hope of God—and a friend. *But what can friends do when a girl's father is in trouble, or has a pack of vicious dogs?*

Five

Clubhouse Fun

When Ally got home, she looked up Sarah's phone number. She wanted to assure her new friend that no one was mad at her. Should she risk a call? She could always hang up if Mr. Matthews answered.

Ally imagined Sarah's dad probably posted guards along his fence, made a hobby of harassing trespassers, and issued commands to his family and their friends, since he couldn't run the world. Gritting her teeth, she ran into the house and dialed the number.

A girl's voice answered. "Hello?"

"Sarah?"

"Yes?"

"This is Ally—Ally O'Connor."

"Oh, hi." Sarah immediately lowered her voice.

"I was just . . . well, you know . . . I wanted you to know we weren't mad at you or anything."

"Oh," Sarah said, sighing. "I was worried. My dad can be mean, but he's not bad all the time. You have to get to know him."

"I'm not sure any of us want to get to know him, if you know what I mean."

"I don't blame you," Sarah said.

"Well, I just wanted to tell you we want you to know we're your friends," Ally added, "and to say that we'll see you at practice tomorrow. I hope you'll do some more stuff on the uneven bars."

"Oh, I will."

"Do you want to be a gymnast?"

"That's been my dream since the Olympics a few years ago."

Ally grinned. "I have a video of the '84 Olympics when Mary Lou Retton won the gold medal. Come over, and we can watch it sometime."

"Oh, I love watching her, too, and especially the Chinese and Russians and, well, all of them. We don't have cable, but we rent videos sometimes—if my dad lets me. He's not really interested though."

"Well, it's good he lets you go to practice."

Ally liked listening to Sarah's voice. But when Sarah said nothing more, Ally said, "See you tomorrow."

"Sure."

At least Sarah wasn't mad. That was a relief. Ally hoped Sarah's dad wasn't mad at Sarah either because of everyone who showed up at the house. Before she could get too lost in this thought trail, the phone rang. It was Nick.

"Hey," Nick said, "let's try again to invite Sarah over. Maybe we could get her to hang out on Saturday if she asks her father instead of *us* asking him."

"Good idea," Ally said. "I don't think he likes us at all."

"What gave you that idea?" Nick teased.

"Okay," Ally said. "Let's ask her at the gym tomorrow. Maybe it'll be different if we don't show up on his property. Maybe he'll let Sarah come if we let her handle asking him. She's says he's not that bad when you get to know him."

The next day, Nick didn't waste time asking Sarah to come over on Saturday. Sarah was delighted because she knew her dad planned to be gone that day anyway. He often went to the neighboring town on weekends for farm supplies.

Nick, Ally, John, and Molly waited that afternoon by the road when Sarah's mother drove up in a ramshackle blue Buick. Sarah jumped out and the kids took her to the clubhouse where they feasted on cupcakes and juice. After playing several games, Molly asked, "Hey, want to go swimming?"

"Yeah, let's!" shouted John and Nick.

Ally looked at Sarah.

"Oh, I bet you didn't bring a bathing suit," she said.

"No," Sarah said.

"You can wear one of mine," Molly said. "Come on, let's change."

Sarah froze. "No, I can't go swimming. I'm sorry."

"It's okay," Ally offered. "Molly has some suits that'll fit you."

Sarah said evenly and low, "I can't go swimming." The way she said it made everyone feel uneasy.

"It's okay," Ally said. "We don't have to go swimming. We can just go out in the boat instead. How 'bout that?"

Everyone nodded. Sarah hung her head. "I'm sorry," she murmured. "I don't want to spoil your party."

"Nothing's spoiled," Nick said, balling up a wrapper and aiming it into the picnic basket. "Let's go out in the boat. I didn't want to go swimming that much anyway."

Suddenly, Sarah was crying. "I'm sorry. I'm really sorry."

Everyone crowded around her. "Hey, it's okay. We don't want to go swimming," John said.

"Don't worry about it," Ally added.

"Water's dirty anyway!" Molly said, shrugging.

Great big tears dripped off Sarah's chin. "I know I'm ruining everything! I know it!"

"No, you're not," Ally said, putting her arm over Sarah's shoulders. "We just didn't know you couldn't go, that's all. It's no big deal."

Sarah nodded and wiped at her eyes.

Ally gave her a hug. "It's okay," she said. "Whatever's wrong, when you want to talk about it, we're your friends."

The boys climbed down out of the clubhouse and ran toward the lake.

Molly and Ally stayed until Sarah stopped crying. "Listen, Sarah," Ally said, "whatever is wrong, if your father hurts you or anything, we want you to know we'll be here for you. You can talk to us."

The kids gathered at the dock and no one mentioned swimming again. They pulled on lifejackets and started rowing away from shore. They even saw a muskrat right off, and then a groundhog came down to the lake to drink.

Afterwards, when Sarah had gone home again, Nick said to Ally, "I wonder why Sarah wouldn't go swimming."

"Maybe she doesn't know how, Mr. Brilliant!" John interrupted.

Nick gave him a shove. "She doesn't know how? Forget it. She's an athlete. She knows how."

Ally couldn't help but think out loud: "At the gym she dresses in the shower stall even though the rest of us change right in the open by the lockers. . . ."

"Well, I can understand that," Molly said. "She's just modest."

"Well, I get the feeling she's hiding something," Ally said.

"Like what?" Molly asked, now curious.

"I don't know. Maybe she has a big mole or something," Ally answered. Suddenly, she didn't want to reveal what she was thinking and what she feared.

"Maybe a birthmark, like me," Nick said laughing.

Ally shrugged. "A lot of people don't like swimming. My mom doesn't. She just likes to lay on the beach."

"Yeah," Nick said. "I bet she has a birthmark."

40

"I think we should find out the truth," Ally said, "so we can help Sarah."

%

That night Ally called Sarah one more time. "It was fun having you at the clubhouse today," Ally said, relieved when Sarah answered.

But Sarah changed the tone of her voice suddenly and said, "No, I'm sorry, we don't need any of those."

"What?"

"I'm sorry, my father is eating dinner and can't come to the phone right now."

"Sarah, what are you talking about?"

In the background, Ally suddenly heard Mr. Matthews bellow, "Just hang up!" Then he swore about the telemarketers who never give up.

"Sorry," Sarah said to Ally, hanging up.

As Ally put down the phone, she realized Sarah had been using her end of the conversation to make it sound like the phone call was from someone else.

"Something is definitely wrong," she said to herself.

The next day, Sarah wasn't at practice.

Or the next.

On Wednesday Ally got the group together. "We have to talk to Sarah."

"Why?" Molly asked.

"You know how she loves practice! But she hasn't been here, and I bet she's hurt. I bet her father has hurt her so she can't come back until her bruises start to fade. Maybe he found out she came to our clubhouse last weekend."

"What do we do then?" Nick said.

"We could pray, like Mom told us," Molly suggested.

"Yes," Ally said. "We should pray . . . and we should show her that she really does have friends. But we have to talk to her in person."

41

The Truth Becomes Apparent

John pulled hard on the string and then threw the kite up in the air. Nick grabbed the string and took off running. The boys, Molly, and Ally had taken their kites with them on the road next to the Matthews's farm. They thought by following the wind they could find an excuse to go onto the property again and see Sarah.

John's kite whipped into the air, flapping in the stiff wind.

"Let's ask Sarah if she wants to come out and fly the kite," Molly said.

"Who goes?" Ally asked.

"Not me," said John. "I'm afraid of dog packs."

"And I have to fly the kite," Nick yelled, tugging on the line.

"I'll shoot you for it," Molly said.

Ally lifted her hand. "Odds?"

"One-two-three," Molly said.

Both girls brought down their hands. Ally held out one finger; Molly two.

"Odds it is," Molly said. "Guess I have to go."

"No," Ally said. "Odds means I get to go."

Molly smiled. "Really?"

"Pray like there ain't no tomorrow!" Ally said, seeing the relief on Molly's face. Then she headed for the gate.

The two boys got the kite flying high in the sky. Ally jogged down the road toward the Matthews's house, her heart pounding with fear. She heard the dogs barking from far away and stopped running. Everything inside her wanted to turn and run back to the gate. Then a calm came over her.

Keeping an eye on the barn, Ally remembered that if you turn from vicious animals or look them in the eye, they're more likely to attack you. She decided to stay put and avoid looking them in the eye. The dogs appeared and started toward her, snarling and yapping. Ally stood still and called out, "Hey, Willie. Good dog. Stay, Willie, stay." The dogs stopped and suddenly fell quiet. Ally moved slowly forward, inching toward the house. Before long she was standing at the farmhouse door and gave it three quick little raps.

Mrs. Matthews, looking tired and pale, opened the door.

"Hi," Ally said, trying to glance around the petite woman's frame. "I was wondering if Sarah . . . "

"Sarah isn't here," Mrs. Matthews said. "I'm sorry." She looked back over her shoulder, then suddenly back at the door, her face twisted as if in pain. "So sorry!" she cried, pushing shut the door.

Ally knocked again, hard.

Mrs. Matthews opened the door a crack. "You can't come here," she said, apologetically. "You must leave—now."

Ally stood in shocked silence, then turned and walked slowly back to the road. The dogs followed silently at her heels, but Ally was more afraid for Sarah than she was afraid of the dogs.

℘

Nick, Molly, and John stopped flying their kites and decided to climb an oak tree off the property where they could watch Sarah's house through binoculars. The house looked forgotten and foreboding, as it had the first time they saw it. But something snaking up the drive distracted their attention—a truck roared through the gate and into the driveway.

"Mr. Matthews!" Nick exclaimed.

"Sarah's in the truck with him," John said, zeroing in with the binoculars. The truck stormed up the dirt road, sending up billows of dust and dirt. John handed the binoculars to Ally, who had just finished telling everyone about Mrs. Matthews.

She honed in on the truck as it cranked into the yard. Suddenly the driver's-side door was thrust open. Mr. Matthews climbed out. He yelled something, but Ally couldn't hear what it was. Sarah's door opened slowly. Mr. Matthews hurried around the back of the truck.

To Ally's horror, he grabbed Sarah and slapped her across the face.

"Did you see that?" Ally cried.

"Yeah," Nick said. "That guy is dangerous."

Beyond them, Sarah started to back away from her dad, but as she turned to leave, Mr. Matthews kicked her in the side. Ally was stunned. She felt afraid for Sarah, so afraid that for a moment she felt paralyzed, unable to move. Then Nick banged his fist on the tree trunk.

"That does it," he shouted. "Let's go get that crumb!"

"Wait," Ally said, pulling Nick back. "Look."

Sarah had run into the house and her mother appeared at the door. Mrs. Matthews stepped out and yelled at Mr. Matthews. He snarled back, then started toward her. But she quickly spun and scurried back into the house, slamming shut the door. Mr. Matthews was tugging at it, cursing and yelling.

"Man, that guy is crazy!" Molly cried.

"Let's get going!" Nick said, swinging down the tree branches.

"Where to?" Everyone clamored down after him.

"To tell him we're going to report him."

"We can't do that!" Ally said. "We should just call the police right now, instead of warning him."

"The police won't be out here until later when everything's calmed down anyway," Nick said fiercely. "Then they won't be able to do anything."

Ally wasn't so sure, but followed anyway, Molly and John close behind. They marched across the yard toward the road, and when they reached it, stopped, staring a moment.

"Remember," Nick said, "we can face any giant."

"Stay calm and don't look the dogs in the eye," Ally advised. "Don't hurry and don't make any sudden movements."

"At least maybe we can keep her dad from hitting her more," offered Molly.

Walking toward the barnyard, Ally felt her knees shaking. She didn't relish the idea of Mr. Matthews hitting anyone. The dogs ran out, barking as usual, and Ally stepped forward, hands in her pockets, saying, "Nice dog. Follow me, guys. Stay, doggie. Nice dog. Talk to them." Before they made it all the way, the front door ripped open, and Mr. Matthews barreled out.

Nick stepped out. "We saw what you did. We're reporting you if you don't stop hitting Sarah."

45

Mr. Matthews leaned right into Nick's face. "I thought I told you not to mess with my business," he said. "I'll tear you apart. Now get out of here before I drag you out."

"We want to see Sarah!" Nick said, working to keep his voice calm and low. "We want to see if she's all right!"

Ally stepped up closer to Nick. She felt a little braver, but the hulking Mr. Matthews loomed over them like a true giant. His breath smelled like a tavern. Ally remembered when her father had once gone into a bar at a restaurant to get change for a telephone while she waited at the cash register. The smell made her feel nauseous.

Mr. Matthews whipped around. "Sarah! Sarah! Get out here. Tell these kids you don-n-n't wanna be friends with 'em!" The edges of his words slid around his tongue.

Sarah appeared in the doorway, red-eyed and frightened.

"Sarah!" Nick said stepping forward. "Are you okay?"

She didn't move.

"Tell these no-gooders to get!" Mr. Matthews said from behind his daughter now. "Tell 'em to keep away! Do it, girl!"

Sarah murmured something.

Nick said, "Sarah, we saw what he did to you."

"He didn't do anything," Sarah mumbled. "I'm all right. Go away."

"Sarah!" Ally cried. "You don't mean that!"

"I do!" Sarah screamed. "Just go away! I don't need your help!"

Mr. Matthews glowered from the background at Ally and Nick, but Molly moved forward this time.

"Sarah, we saw what happened," Molly said. "We . . ."

"Nothing happened!" Sarah wailed. She opened the door a crack. "Hear that? Nothing happened! Now go away. You're not my friends anymore!" Huge tears welled into her eyes and slid down her cheeks. She turned to go inside, shutting the door behind her.

"You heard her," Mr. Matthews sputtered. "Now get!" He kicked dirt at Nick and Ally. Molly jumped back, but John came forward.

"I'm not letting you do this!" he said.

The big man shoved John five feet away into the dirt, and laughed. "Who's next?"

No one moved. Mr. Matthews flashed a self-satisfied smirk, and his heavy breathing left an odor of stale tobacco mixed with alcohol.

"Please! Please leave! Just leave!" Sarah cried. "It'll be worse for me if you don't go!" She was face-to-face at the screen door with Ally. "Do you understand? It'll be worse— for me! Please."

"Sarah, I told you to get inside," her father growled slowly.

Sarah blinked, then backed from the door, into that sorry house. Her mother, in the shadows, reached for her with open arms.

Nick and Ally stepped down from the porch.

Mr. Matthews was grinning triumphantly. "See, I told you she doesn't want you around," he said with a little shrug. "You're stickin' your nose into the wrong business. Now if you don't get off my property it's me who's goin' to call the cops, get my drift?"

Mr. Matthews turned and shambled off to his truck as if nothing was wrong. John was still lying in the dirt. Molly and Ally helped him to his feet. They all hurried back down the driveway, angry and shocked.

"What do we do now?" Ally whispered.

Molly sniffled then burst into tears.

Nick leaned close to Molly and said, "It's all right. We tried to help."

"But should we just leave?" Ally wondered aloud.

"For now what else can we do?" Nick said. "You heard them. Sarah doesn't want to talk to us, and her dad aims to hurt us."

"I don't think that's true," Ally said, "about Sarah." She frowned, lost somewhere in thought, then fell silent. Nick stayed quiet too. Only Molly sniffled and John moaned with each step that became a slight limp.

Reaching home, Ally left the somber group. "See you guys later," she said, watching the others disappear down the street. Closing the front door behind her, Ally's own tears then began to fall.

Seven

The Kids Wonder What to Do

Ally tried to pray, but the upset of the afternoon kept interrupting and stirring her thoughts. She pulled out her Bible and searched for a passage that might help her think how to help Sarah. When she heard the front door open and shut, she carried her Bible into the living room where her dad was sorting through the mail. Ally spilled out the story of Sarah.

"You're sure?" Ally's father asked, setting down the mail. "You saw her father hit her? This is the kind of thing that should be reported to the state social services. Mother or daughter have to press the charges. But first I'm more concerned with you confronting Mr. Matthews like that. Especially if the man physically accosted John. That should be reported to the police."

"No," Ally cried. "Sarah said that would only end up hurting her more. Mr. Matthews might get angrier and take it out on his wife and Sarah."

Ally's father nodded understandingly, but his brows were knitted in concern.

"It seems like Sarah wants us to stay out of it," Ally told him.

"Well, that may be true," Ally's dad said finally. "But there are several ways to approach this. The first is to put more pressure on this Mr. Matthews. We can call the police and have them investigate. Second, we can talk to social services, offer evidence, and hope they do their own investigation. But, of course, this is Sarah's family, and it might alienate her more. The main thing is to keep friendship with Sarah, because that's the most important way we can help her right now. If you push the issue with the police, Mr. Matthews may take his family and leave the state."

"Or, she might not tell the truth to the police!" Ally wondered aloud.

"Yes," her father cautioned. "It's really odd, but people who have been hurt the most don't always recognize that it's wrong. They think that's just the way it is because they've never known anything else. They don't realize that love doesn't hurt, so they cover up for the people ruining their lives."

"It did seem like Sarah was trying to protect her father," Ally admitted.

"We don't know what's happened in the past, either," her dad said, sighing. "Maybe Sarah had this trouble before. Maybe she's been taken away from her parents, and knows what it's like to be a foster kid—all the insecurity and worry, going from home to home, never really feeling a part of anything. That can be a horrible life, even for the most loving and forgiving person like Sarah seems to be."

50

"Then what *can* we do?" Ally slumped into a living room chair in resignation.

"A third option is to just love her exactly as things are," Mr. O'Connor said. "Win Sarah by your friendship, not your interference. See if she eventually talks to you about the abuse. If she'll talk to you, then she'll talk to the authorities. Win Sarah's trust and show her that getting help can only turn out for good—for her father, too."

Ally nodded slowly, still sorting out the advice.

"By the way, could it be possible that Mr. Matthews is addicted to alcohol?" Mr. O'Connor gently prodded.

"Well," Ally ventured, feeling more miserable than ever, "he slurs his words sometimes, and his breath reeks."

"That could be part of it, though you can't be too sure," Mr. O'Connor said.

Ally felt a lot of love for her father. He always encouraged her, even though he and her mom had their own difficulties. *If only Sarah could rely on her father like this,* Ally thought, then she asked, "Dad, why does God let these kinds of things happen? Why doesn't he fix them when we pray?"

Mr. O'Connor smiled. "You're asking the question of the ages, honey. Everyone has asked that question at one time or another. I guess it all goes back to the story of the Good Samaritan."

"I know that one," Ally said.

"The Samaritan didn't know what happened to the man who had been robbed and beaten, or why. He just stepped in and helped. That's the essence of love. You don't have to know all the reasons behind something, but just believe that if you meet someone who needs help, then your path has crossed their path for a reason."

"Like Sarah," Ally said.

"Well, your friend Sarah needs help," her father said. "But she might not need the kind of help you want to give. You kids shouldn't be confronting her father by yourselves. Keep your eyes open, but stay out of the way of that man.

51

He could get more violent with you. Let God work; the Lord will bring everything around to a place where you can help Sarah in an unexpected way. Ask God to soften Mr. Matthews's heart, and to help Sarah speak the truth."

Ally sighed. "So we should try to get a little closer to Sarah and pray every day that God will work?"

"That's what I'd do," her father said. "That's what friendship is all about."

"That's what I want to be," Ally said. "Sarah's friend."

∾

The next day at practice Sarah acted aloof. She didn't speak to anyone, just kept to herself and concentrated on her routines.

Ally couldn't stand pretending nothing had happened. After working on the balance beam, she went up to Sarah. "I'm sorry," she said quietly. "I hope we didn't make things worse for you last night." There was so much more she wanted to say, but Ally bit her lip. She thought if she said too much, it would just drive Sarah away.

Sarah nodded, businesslike. "There's nothing you can do."

"We just want to be your friends."

"I don't know whether my father will let me be friends with you guys right now," Sarah said, looking at the floor.

"Does he arrange your friendships?" Ally realized she sounded more alarmed than she intended. "Don't you have anything to say about it?" she asked more gently.

"Not right now."

Something in the way Sarah answered broke Ally's heart. Sarah sounded so final and defeated. "Sarah, just remember we're here for you. I hate to think of you ever being hurt or scared; I believe you should tell someone who can help. Whatever you do, I still want to be your friend."

"Nothing is wrong, Ally."

"Okay. Whatever you say."

Mr. James interrupted the girls, calling Sarah: "Come and work with some of these other kids. I think they might get it if you show them a few things."

Sarah turned to Ally before crossing the gym. "Please don't talk to anyone about this," she pleaded. "Nothing serious happened, and if it did, it will only mean more trouble for me."

"Okay," Ally promised, "don't worry, Sarah. I won't and I'll tell Nick not to either."

Sarah stepped over to the mats and demonstrated a handspring. Then she helped other teammates get the hang of it. Ally tried several herself, then concentrated most of her time back on the uneven bars. She was learning to kip up on the lower bar, swing over it, and leap to the higher bar. It wasn't that hard, just a little scary at first.

After gymnastics practice everyone collapsed on the mats while Mr. James talked about their progress. "Each of you will need to get permission from your parents to participate in the meets," he said. "They need to sign this form." He handed a stack of legal looking papers to Nick who passed them around. Before even reading the sheet Nick handed her, Ally immediately wondered about Sarah. *Will her father allow her to be a part of it?*

"We have a lot of talent here," Mr. James said. "I can already see that. We can go far. If we win just six of our meets, we'll end up going to the county finals. From there, it's the state finals. Some of you could even go on to the nationals.

"First let's determine which of you do best on which pieces of equipment. This will take some time, so hang in there. We'll all be going places. Okay? Let's hear a cheer!"

Everyone shouted "Go Jaguars," and then kept up the spirit even after Coach James dismissed practice.

Walking home, Ally told Nick, Molly, and John of Sarah's request. Ally also shared her father's advice.

"But how can we be friends if Sarah won't let us?" Molly asked.

"That's what we have to figure out," Ally answered. "The way I see it, we stick with the gymnastics team, root for Sarah, and be kind and supportive of her, even if she doesn't act friendly back. I don't think we should sweat it. If she wants to be friends, she'll come around. We don't have to force it. We have to win her trust. Remember the key word is 'win'!"

"It's not that simple," Nick said, stopping. He seemed so serious all of a sudden. "She's not being this way because she wants to be," he said. "Her father is forcing her. We don't know what she really thinks about any of these things because she hasn't said."

"Yeah," Molly whispered.

"But maybe we just need to give her time," Ally ventured.

"Maybe we need to be around more of the time," Nick interrupted. "I don't know about you all, but I'm going to keep an eye on things—and I'm going to start now. Sarah's farm is just down that road and it's hours before dinner-time. I'm going to pass by."

Reluctantly Ally and Molly followed. Ally wanted to give Sarah space, but, like Nick, she found it hard to just keep away from a friend in need.

The three fell into silence as they walked toward Sarah's farm. It was a beautiful day: quiet, still, if only faintly spoiled by the acrid scent of smoke and something burning somewhere.

Something was burning, straight ahead. Ally noticed smoke! She motioned for Nick and Molly to watch two figures moving through the grass near the beehives. A tall person and one half in size, each wearing a veil, crept slowly through the apple orchard close to the road.

"It's Mr. Matthews and Sarah in beekeeping clothing," Nick whispered. "Look! He's got a smoker. They're going to get the honey." He pulled Ally, Molly, and John behind some trees to watch.

Mr. Matthews had what looked like a little tent of netting on his head, and what looked like a toolbox in one hand. In his other hand was the strangest contraption Ally had ever seen: a barrel with a sort of accordian on the back and a blow-dryer-like mouth at the top, from which smoke billowed.

"Watch," Nick whispered. "Those bees will be ornery. They won't like him stealing their honey. But the smoker will make them sleepy so they won't sting."

Mr. Matthews set the smoking machine under the beehive and waited several minutes. Sarah opened a door on the reverse side of the hive. Mr. Matthews used an extractor tool to fill a bucket with the sticky honey and honeycomb.

"I bet it's scrumptious," Nick said.

"Want to try some?" John asked. "Just go ask for a lick."

"Yeah, right," Molly interjected, "and get stung from head to toe."

John laughed. "I'd like to see that. Right on the behind! That would be great."

"For you, maybe," Nick said with a chuckle.

Mr. Matthews and Sarah had finished with the beehive, closed it up, and started back up the hill. There were several other beehives in the orchard, but they ignored them.

"Do you think they sell the honey?" Nick wondered aloud. "What do you think they could make from honey like that?"

"Honey's not very expensive at the supermarket," Ally said, watching Sarah and her father disappear over a hill. "Seems like a tough way to make a buck."

The thought lingered in the air with the scent of the honey that had just been exposed. The kids sat for a long time just enjoying the sun on their backs and the breeze. They were about to leave when they heard the pounding of horse's hooves.

"Hey!" Sarah called. She sat on Colonel, looking tiny in comparison.

"Sarah!" Ally called. "You look like quite a horsewoman!"

"My dad usually lets me ride Colonel after I help him with the bees," she smiled. It was the first smile Ally had seen from Sarah since that day they met at the gym and Sarah was engrossed in a routine on the bars.

"So you're all right?" Nick asked.

"Look," Sarah said, leaning down to whisper, "I'm fine. It's been a good day—"

A booming voice from behind interrupted. "Get back up here, Sarah!"

She whipped around, wheeled the horse, and galloped back toward her father on the other side of the hill.

"Does he ever let her breathe?" Nick complained as Colonel kicked up puffs of dirt on the road.

Eight

A Plan Is Conceived

The next day at practice Coach James asked Ally if she'd talk to Sarah about the team forms and plans. "It's strange," he said. "I thought she'd be the first one to return it. Her father let her come to the practices, and I told him personally I believed Sarah was a great gymnast. He knew if she was to compete, a parent had to sign these forms."

"Well, I think Sarah could win most of the medals," Ally commented. "I'll remind her about the form."

But that morning Sarah showed up late and went through practice silently. Ally thought Sarah seemed worried about something. She didn't even perk up when Nick tried to crack one of his jokes.

"How are you today, Sarah?" Ally asked when they got a moment alone, between events.

"Okay, I guess."

Ally leaned on her chair. "Has your Mom or Dad signed that form?"

Sarah didn't respond.

"Sarah, you're going to compete with us, aren't you?"

"I . . . don't know, . . ." Sarah said, her voice trailing off.

"You're the best one on the team, Sarah. We need you for the meets."

"I said I don't know." Sarah's jaw was set. She stayed away, and Ally knew Sarah was upset. Ally laid her hand on Sarah's shoulder. "Did your dad say you couldn't do it?"

Sarah bit her lip and didn't respond right away. Then she sighed. "Yeah, he says I have too many chores to do. I don't have time."

"But you're the best. . . ."

"Ally," Sarah said. "I can't go against my dad. He's my dad, even if he doesn't make sense sometimes."

Ally stooped down next to her. "What if you had some help or something? What if we helped you do your chores?"

"At six-thirty in the morning?"

"We wake up early. We'd love to help." Ally beamed. "We'll help you any way we can." She surveyed the room. "Nick," she called, "come here a minute!"

"Nick! Molly!"

"Ally!" Sarah protested. "Please, you mean well, but—"

"Molly, come here!"

Ally smiled up at Sarah. "Look, we can help you with the chores. It's that simple. We want you to be on this team. We need you! You could make it the best. You're great at everything. We'll all help."

"It's the money!" Sarah suddenly said. "My dad doesn't have the money."

"Seventy-five dollars?"

At times in Ally's life, seventy-five dollars seemed like a fortune. There were a lot of clothes, shoes, books, and other things you could buy with seventy-five dollars. But if her father didn't make her earn the money herself, he'd usually sign a check to make up the difference of whatever Ally needed for things that were purposeful. Anyway, Ally knew her parents could afford paying for gymnastics.

"My dad just doesn't have a lot of money," Sarah said.

Ally had an idea: Maybe her mom and dad could pay for Sarah. Or maybe she, Nick, and the team could collect the money needed.

"We'll earn the money," she told Sarah.

"My dad isn't on welfare," Sarah said, for the first time looking up into Ally's eyes. "He won't take that either."

Nick walked over. "Hi, Sarah," he said.

"Hi, Nick," Sarah murmured with a blush.

"What's up?"

"Sarah's dad won't let her compete," Ally said, explaining the situation. "She has to do chores every morning and afternoon. Can't we help?"

Nick grinned. "Help you do your chores? Sure. I always wanted to work on a farm!"

"They have to be done really early in the morning," Sarah said, obviously warming up.

"Hey, the early bird gets the worm, right?" Nick said.

"But I still can't come up with the money," Sarah said.

Nick grinned. "Hey, your dad harvests honey, right?"

"Oh, there's not that much of it," Sarah said. "He does sell some. He never talks about it."

"What if we ask your father to let you sell it at practice?" Nick asked. "We could have a special team sale. At less than the market price, all you'd have to do is sell twenty or so jars to cover the gym fee—and the families of everyone on the team would buy that much because everyone wants you with us."

"You—talk to my father?" Sarah said. "No way. If it's to be done, I'd better do it."

"Please, let us come with you. We won't say anything," Ally said.

"No, my dad's already too mad at you," Sarah said, shaking her head.

"But he might turn just you down," Nick said. "And maybe we can come up with something that can win him over to see how good this would be for you. He'd be the father of a champion."

The coach suddenly noticed the kids standing around Sarah. "What's going on, folks?" he asked.

Sarah looked up in fear, but Ally quietly explained Sarah's predicament and their idea.

Coach James rubbed his chin. "Sounds like a winner of an idea to me. Do you think your dad would agree, Sarah? What if I wrote him a note? I could even supervise the honey harvesting. I used to do it on my uncle's farm, growing up. It's been a long time, but I still remember it all like yesterday."

"You would do all that?" Sarah said, looking hopeful for the first time. "A note from you would help." She paused. "But it won't be easy. My dad doesn't like strangers, and I'm not sure what he'd think of you working around his bees!"

"All right, let me compose a note," Coach James said, "and we'll just see."

Everyone nodded. Ally remembered the special auction the church had sponsored where parents and kids volunteered special services, cakes and desserts, and other things like sports equipment for special prices. Some kids volunteered to clean the buyer's house, some offered to do all the windows in the spring, and others sold services like cutting lawns and edging them. John had even photographed some portraits for one family. All these little services had been auctioned off for different prices, and the auction ended up being a great way to bring in money to purchase some camping equipment for the youth group. *Good things always happen when people work together,* Ally thought.

"We'll go talk to your dad this afternoon with Coach James's letter," Nick told Sarah.

"And what if he still doesn't let me participate?" Sarah said.

"Well, then at least you'll have tried," Molly said.

Nick gave the group a firm thumbs-up. "It's gonna work," he said. "You'll see."

☙

Walking up the dirt road to the Matthews's farm after practice, Sarah seemed more excited than Ally had ever seen her.

"Now let me get my dad in a good mood before he talks to you," Sarah said. "And whatever you do, don't argue with him. If he doesn't like something, just go along with it. Understand?"

Nick, Molly, and John nodded as Ally looked each of them in the eyes and said, "Yes, Sarah, we understand. Remember we're here as your friends."

When they entered the farmyard the dogs began barking and running. Sarah sprinted ahead to quiet them. Ally followed to show she wasn't afraid anymore. In fact she'd nearly made friends with Willie.

"Diplomacy!" Nick said. "Diplomatic relations is my specialty."

"Nick is always speaking another language," Molly interrupted, rolling her eyes.

"Diplomatic relations is how nations talk to one another," Nick said. "It's usually done through ambassadors. They talk and get things worked out before the big boys—the presidents—discuss things. It's the way people who disagree start to come together."

Ally interrupted, "I think we'd better get ready. Look, there he is."

Mr. Matthews rode out on Colonel.

"All right, everybody, be cool," Nick whispered.

They ambled up to Mr. Matthews, but before anyone could utter a word, he said, "Sarah, I told you to stay away . . ."

"Dad," Sarah said with some newfound courage. "My gymnastics coach asked Ally and Nick to bring you this note. Would you read it?" She held the note from Coach James out to her father.

He took it, scanned it quickly, and asked, "So?"

"Well, Nick wants to say something."

Mr. Matthews turned with hard eyes at Nick.

"Sir," Nick said, stepping out in front, "we want to apologize for our conduct the last few days."

Mr. Matthews just stared at Nick with that same hard look, but Ally could see his face softening slightly.

"We know we were wrong to interfere," Nick said. "We want to make up for that."

"So what are you sayin'? Are you finally gonna stay out of my business?"

"Yes," Nick said, "and we also want to be good neighbors." There was an uncomfortable pause as Mr. Matthews stirred in the saddle. Nick seized the opportunity. "That's quite a horse," he told Mr. Matthews.

"Horses are God's greatest creatures," Mr. Matthews said with pride. "Colonel here is one of the best. He comes from a long line of thoroughbreds. I expect his line to win races."

"He certainly is a fine one. You picked him well," Nick said.

Mr. Matthews chuckled. "You butterin' me up?"

Nick shook his head. "I'm just admiring your horse, sir. But it's true we did come here to ask your permission. We understand Sarah wants to compete with our gymnastics team, and we have a proposal you might find interesting."

Ally almost laughed. Where did Nick dream up this stuff? Sarah's mother came outside, and Ally overheard Sarah whisper to her mother, "They're good friends to me, aren't they?"

Her mother nodded.

"What you tryin' to say, boy? Spit it out!" Mr. Matthews said.

Nick said, "This is our way of saying, 'Let bygones be bygones.'"

Mr. Matthews asked, "What's the kicker?"

"We wish, sir," Nick said, reminding Ally of an English courtier from a novel she'd read, "that your daughter, Sarah, would be allowed to compete with our gymnastics team."

"Uh-huh!" Mr. Matthews exclaimed.

Nick glanced at Ally, then John, as if for help.

Ally stepped forward. "Mr. Matthews, what we're trying to say is that we're willing to help Sarah with the chores, and we're willing to raise the money to help Sarah pay the fee. We know it's a lot, and we're used to working to earn money for things we want."

"And how do you propose to do that?" Mr. Matthews said. His broad, tanned face almost glowed with mirth, but it made Ally angry. Then, suddenly she realized that for the first time they were talking civilly to Mr. Matthews. She decided she'd just plow on.

"We thought, sir—" Ally said, but Nick spoke over her.

"What we had in mind, sir," Nick said, winking at Ally, "is to help you harvest your honey. There's enough for you, we think, in the several hives you have, and enough more for Sarah to bottle up and sell to team members. We figure it'll take about twenty jars to make seventy-five dollars at four dollars apiece, and . . ."

"Not if I take 50 percent!" Mr. Matthews exclaimed. "And why should I let you take honey from my beehives?"

"It's not me," Nick said. "It's for Sarah—Sarah will harvest the honey with Mr. James's help. And yes, we will give you 50 percent."

Mrs. Matthews stepped out of the shadows, where she'd been listening from a distance. "Please," she begged. "Let them do this. For Sarah."

Mr. Matthews scowled slightly, then said, "Where do you think you kids will get all those jars you'll need?"

Nick stood up. "We thought you'd . . ."

"Oh, I'm not going to provide the jars! That's extra money. You buy your own jars. You get the honey, and you sell it. I get 50 percent of the profits. That's my final word." He turned to Sarah and said sternly, "If you sell enough of the honey to give me seventy-five dollars, I'll let you do the gymnastics for the other seventy-five. But you still have to do your chores! Every single day!"

Sarah's mother stepped forward. "I have extra jars," she said, smiling nervously. "From canning."

Mr. Matthews shook his head with exasperation but said nothing.

"I'll do the chores, Dad," Sarah said. "Thank you. Thank you." She ran past her father into the barn. Nick, Ally, Molly, and John followed and scurried inside.

Mr. Matthews watched them with wide eyes, then shook his head.

Ally smiled. They'd convinced Mr. Matthews of their friendship, but he did drive a difficult bargain! Now they had a big problem: How were they ever going to sell one hundred and fifty dollars' worth of honey? Was there even that much in the hives?

Nine

The Honey Story

On the way home, Nick told Ally, "We need a bush hat and some mosquito netting to put over it to protect us from the bees when we go after the honey. I know just where to get those things."

That evening Nick and his dad went to the surplus store, where they purchased several yards of mosquito netting to go over Nick's Australian Outback bush hat.

Mr. Parker asked, "You're sure this is what you want?"

"Yeah," Nick said. "Coach James said it'll work fine, and it's cheap. We wear leather work gloves and thick downy jackets and tight-weave pants with the hat. The netting drapes down and tucks into our neck so the bees can't get in."

"I'm not sure about this, Nick. You've never harvested honey before. You may be getting in over your head. Bee stings can be dangerous."

"Coach James is a pro. He's going to help us. And I read all about it in a book anyway."

"Will the bees follow you?" Mr. Parker asked.

"For a little ways," Nick said. "But if you cover up the honey, they forget."

❧

The next day after practice, Ally and John gathered with Molly and Nick in their driveway. "All we've got to do now," Nick told them as he showed them how to dress like a beekeeper, "is meet Coach James at the farm."

They walked to Sarah's house in high spirits, excited to help their new friend. Nick seemed especially anxious, walking a little ahead the whole way and then stepping up to knock on the door.

"Hi," Sarah answered. "Coach James is already here. Let's go to the barn and get ready."

"Yes, if I'm going to get stung," Nick told her with bravado, "I'd rather get it over with."

"What do you mean?" Ally asked. "I thought you were wearing all this so you wouldn't get stung."

"Well," Nick said, "chances are just one or two bees will get through the netting somehow, or crawl up my jacket. If I run or get flustered, I might lose the netting and then be totally open to attack."

Nick Parker, you're braver than I imagined, Ally thought as she followed everyone to the barn where Sarah put on her beekeeping gear. Coach James determined Nick and Sarah should be the only ones to actually pull honey out of the hives. Sarah had experience and Nick had studied bee-keeping. Besides, the coach said as he pulled on Mr. Matthews's beekeeper headdress, too many helpers and they'd all be stumbling over one another.

66

Sarah brought out a large cooler with three square pots inside for the honey. She also produced an extractor, which separated the honey from the honeycomb.

Meanwhile, Coach James demonstrated how to use the smoker right under the hive.

"We'll let it smoke for five or ten minutes," he explained, "to anesthetize the bees and make them less likely to sting. They'll think the smoke means fire, then gorge on the honey, becoming too heavy to fly."

"Then what?" Ally asked.

"Then comes the tricky part," Coach James said. "With the extractor, we'll remove the honey without harming the honeycomb. You see, the hive has three tiers inside, the bottom one with a wax honeycomb in place. If we leave the comb intact, the bees won't have to rebuild the nest and they'll go on with the production of honey like nothing happened."

"Only we'll have the goods," Nick said, popping over Coach James's shoulder with all the necessary tools raised in each hand.

Coach James laughed. "Right," he said. "Let's go."

Ally, John, and Molly followed Coach James and Nick, with Sarah in the lead. She crept toward the hives, gripping the extractor and storage pots. Right behind her Nick carried the smoker, with Coach James close by, talking them through the steps.

Nick placed the smoker under the first hive, lit it, and in seconds heavy smoke was wafting into the air and around the boxlike hive. Soon most of the bee swarm calmed down.

Ally watched with a pair of binoculars as Nick pulled out the lower drawer and Sarah used the extractor to remove the honey. Ally watched it drip into the pans.

"It's going great," she told John and Molly who peered from behind.

❧

"Smoke got them all," Nick said, as he helped Coach James haul the cooler full of honey back to the farmyard.

Sarah laughed. "I bet we got over ten pounds from just one of the six hives."

Ally marveled at how lighthearted Sarah seemed. *Is it because her father isn't in a mood to spoil things or because she has his blessing? But there isn't time to dwell on why now,* she told herself as she followed Molly into the barn. Coach James had asked them to find the large pot Mr. Matthews used for cooking the honey on a gas stove. The heat caused any excess wax to rise to the surface, so they could skim it off, the coach explained; this purified it, leaving the sweet liquid more golden yet clear.

"Watch for the honeycomb," Ally urged Molly. "The more pure we make the honey, the more money we can get for it."

"I know, I know," Molly said, staring down into the large pot where the honey was beginning to bubble. Already Ally saw some of the wax oozing to the surface. She rushed back out into the yard. Down in the orchard, she spotted Nick and Sarah finishing up on the second hive. When they were done, John trundled the honey into the barn, where Molly purified it.

As Coach James and the others finished up the rest of the hives, Ally watched one more time through the binoculars. Everything was going better than they hoped. Everyone was working as a team; there were no problems, no mishaps, no stings. When Sarah and Nick brought up the last batch, they were red and sweaty, but laughing.

"I bet we got thirty pounds," Sarah told Ally. "At five dollars a pound, that's one hundred and fifty dollars."

"If we can sell it for that much," Ally added.

"This is the best kind of honey," Coach James said winking. "It'll sell. Plus, people will gladly buy this from you kids since it's for a worthy project."

They brought the last load into the barn. Molly and John kept the pot hot and bubbling. They continued boiling the honey until no pieces of honeycomb were left in it at all.

"I tasted a little of it," Molly confessed. "It's delicious."

"Plus I have a surprise—my mom has an order for two pounds," Nick announced. "So we're already ahead."

"Yeah, my parents already told me they want to buy some too," Ally said. She licked her lips as she inhaled the sweet aroma of the warm honey. "Mmm," she hummed. "I can't wait to put some on my breakfast toast."

"Put me down for two and any of the rest that you don't sell," Coach James said.

"Oh, Mr. James," Sarah said, "you don't have to."

"I want to, Sarah. Imagine this good honey all winter long!"

Ally and Sarah began pouring the pure honey into the Mason jars sent with them that morning from each of their mothers. Ally had watched her mom boil the jars to sterilize them along with the lids. Now John and Nick were weighing each one on a scale to price them. By late afternoon thirty-five jars, each containing one and a quarter pounds of honey, had been sealed and marked for sale at six dollars each. "That's more than one hundred and fifty dollars!" Nick said as he inventoried the gleaming, golden stash. "The purest honey is from the bottom, so we could actually price those jars higher. Well, maybe we should pass on that." Coach James took his two jars before leaving, bragging, "Cream of the crop."

"We'll split them up," Nick told Ally. "I'll take half, and Sarah and I can sell them on my street. You and John and Molly can take the other half and sell them on your street. That is, after we've sold what we can to each of our families."

Sarah couldn't stop smiling. "You're the greatest friends I ever had."

"GFA. Great Friends Anonymous," Nick said. "That's us."

"Yeah, right," Ally said, rolling her eyes. "We're so anonymous."

"And humble!" Molly quipped.

Nick laughed. "So much for GFA," he whispered to Sarah, then said to the others, "anyway, let's plan to sell as much honey as we can tomorrow morning. Then how about we all meet at the clubhouse."

"I'll be there as soon as I get my chores done," Sarah said.

"I'll help you," Nick promised.

"Me too," Ally said. "I can be here at the crack of dawn."

"No, you've already helped enough," Sarah protested. "Anyway, it's just feeding the chickens, cleaning up after the horse and dogs, and then doing the dishes left from breakfast."

"You sure do have a lot of chores," Ally said, looking at Sarah with wonder. "How do you do it all?"

"If you woke up at five-thirty every morning, suddenly you'd have all the time in the world."

John interrupted, "Hey, we have to get a picture!" He pulled a little camera out of the backpack where he kept all his supplies. "Everyone grab a couple jars of honey and hold them up. Come on, out in front of the barn!"

Everyone giggled and grabbed the golden jars, still warm and scenting the air.

John snapped several photos, and then Ally took his place and got several with him in the picture. Everyone was laughing, joking, and teasing each other. Even Sarah's mom came out and congratulated the GFA in her best English. John took several more pictures of her and Sarah alone, promising to give them each a photo once he developed the film.

Suddenly Mr. Matthews zoomed into the yard in his truck. The dogs rushed out to greet him. Sarah said she'd better show her dad how they'd done so well with the honey.

"Are your chores done, or did you play with the honey first?" Mr. Matthews said, brushing Sarah off with his huge hand.

"I did all the chores, Dad."

Mr. Matthews brightened. "All right. As long as the important work's done. Your friends will have to go now." Reluctantly, Sarah's father signed the gymnastics competition permission papers. He kept saying over and over, "This better not interfere with your chores." Sarah kept assuring him everything would be done even when the competitions started.

Mr. Matthews didn't even look at Nick or the others. Ally thought: *He just doesn't like any of us. Maybe he agreed to the honey harvest because he was going to get 50 percent of the money.* That made Ally mad. *But that was the deal. What else could we do anyway? We had to get Sarah on the team.*

When her father stepped into the house, Sarah shrugged and said, "You guys had better go."

"At least he's letting us be your friends," Nick said.

"We'll see you tomorrow morning," Ally added.

"Right," Nick said then, trying to lighten the mood, added, "Come on, GFA, let's go."

Ten

Hopes Are Dashed

"Who knew that selling the honey from Sarah's farm would be the easiest part of their whole team harvesting venture?" Coach James said the next week at practice. It was going well. When people learned proceeds would help Sarah join the gymnastics team, they bought eagerly, though the honey seemed expensive. Everyone recognized Sarah's natural talent! In no time the thirty-five jars were gone.

But the gymnastics themselves weren't going so well. For everyone on the team, practice became intense. Coach James would start everyone on the mats each session now. Somersaults, rolls, headsprings, and handsprings—each stunt should be strengthened.

Each stunt wasn't so easy though. The handspring was difficult for Molly. She couldn't seem to orient her body enough for the sudden thrust and flip even when Coach James was there to swing her all the way over. Sarah encouraged her and repeatedly talked her through each one: "Set your feet. Run. Leap to your hands—good—and now over . . ."

But whomp! Too many times Molly found herself on her back again.

With determination and with many tries, Molly finally got it, but she still hadn't mastered any flips or somersaults like Sarah's, which seemed so effortless. There was much work to do, Molly knew, hearing Coach James remind even the strong and athletic team members to polish their performances and keep their toes pointed.

When the uniforms and special tumbling shoes arrived during the second week, the girls pranced about in sleek leotards looking for all the world like Olympians. The boys showed off their new physiques in foot-strapped pants and muscle shirts. But everyone knew what was important wasn't how they looked. It was how they performed that mattered now. Only, even after two weeks, things weren't looking as good as Coach James had hoped. Some team members had perfected the handspring, round off, and cartwheel. The outlook on the equipment was dismal though. Sarah remained the only performer. Even Nick lapsed into silence as Coach James gave pep talks and told everyone not to worry about the "crowd-pleasing" moves.

"Just get out there next week and do what you can," he said. "You've all come a long way, and while I know you want to go farther, I'm proud of you right here, right now!"

The third week, however, disaster struck. While performing on the rings Nick overcompensated and pulled a muscle in his shoulder. He was going to be out for the rest of the summer!

The same week Ally nose-dived off the vault—literally—and hurt her nose. Molly worked hard on the mats and suffered no injuries, but it was clear she wasn't the bolster the team needed.

It was in Sarah that everyone put high hopes. She sensed this and pushed herself even farther, becoming even more of a true marvel. On the mats, she could perform six moves in a single fifty-foot span. On the uneven parallel bars, she swung around like a joyous, half-crazed monkey. It was fun just to watch her.

But even this wouldn't last.

Ally was on her way to the girls' bathroom when she heard a shout in the hall.

"You can't barge through like that, sir!" It was Mr. Bellows, the janitor. Stalking ahead of him was Sarah's father.

"I'm here to get my daughter," Mr. Matthews growled.

"But sir, you must check in at the office."

"I do *not* need to check in with any office," Mr. Matthews said raising his voice.

Ally stood stock-still. She was afraid to move for fear she'd give Mr. Matthews a clue as to where Sarah was. *But what can Mr. Bellows do?* Ally wondered. Mr. Bellows was half Mr. Matthews's size and twice as old. He rushed after Mr. Matthews, gesturing and waving. "If you'll just follow me to the office, we can help you. Now. who is your daughter, sir?"

"She's practicin'. She didn't do her chores. That was the deal. She has to do her chores."

Ally knew instantly when Mr. Matthews spotted her. "There's one of those kids who's been upsetting things. Hey, you!"

Ally started to push the bathroom door open but knew it was no refuge. Before she got inside the door, Mr. Matthews grabbed her at the shoulder and yanked her back into the hall.

"Where is she?" he demanded.

Mr. Bellows rushed up, his face red and perspiring. "Sir, I'll take you to the gym."

Mr. Matthews paid no attention. He towered over Mr. Bellows like a Kodiak bear over a child, then pulled Ally down the hall. "Take me to her."

"I must protest, sir!" Mr. Bellows cried.

"If she had done her chores, there wouldn't be a problem," Mr. Matthews seethed. "Now there's a problem.

74

Always have a problem with that kid. She's got to get home, and I mean now."

"Good heavens, what chore did she forget?" Mr. Bellows said, momentarily diverted.

"All of them!" Mr. Matthews erupted.

Ally tried to stall, but Mr. Matthews just shoved her ahead of him. "Move it!" he shouted. She forced one leg in front of another with him poking her back. He smelled of sweat and something else. Ally realized suddenly what it was: liquor. She shivered. *What might Sarah's father do to me if he's drunk?*

Mr. Bellows said fiercely, "I will have to call the police, sir."

"Where is she?" was all Mr. Matthews would say.

There was nothing else to do but go directly to the gym where the team was practicing. Ally opened the door and stepped inside. Mr. Matthews stomped along right behind her.

Everyone working on the mats, the side horse, and the uneven bars stopped to stand motionless as Mr. Matthews yelled, "Sarah, get your stuff!"

Coach James stood up and jogged over, urging, over his shoulder, for everyone to keep practicing. "Can I help you?" he asked, breathless in front of Mr. Matthews.

"Get me Sarah—that's how you can help me!" Mr. Matthews bellowed.

Ally watched Sarah, startled, hurry to her dad's side. Nick jumped up from the mats and followed.

"We just started practice," Coach James said. "If you could just let Sarah continue . . ."

"She didn't do her chores."

"I did, Dad!" Sarah said.

Nick gave Ally a look that said, "She's right, but we've got trouble here."

"You didn't. Now get going!" Mr. Matthews grabbed Sarah's hand and wrenched her toward the door.

"Dad, please!" she cried.

But Mr. Matthews plowed ahead, yanking his daughter after him. Sarah stumbled along, looking frantically after Coach James, Ally, and Nick.

Coach James sprang up to follow; Nick and Ally took off after him.

Halfway down the hallway Coach James grasped Sarah's father at the shoulder, and Mr. Matthews whirled around, snarling, "Get your hand off me, man!"

Coach James lowered his voice, but said calmly, "I can't permit you to treat one of my team members this way!"

Mr. Matthews lifted his fist, but Coach James stood his ground.

"I don't want to charge you!" Coach James said. "But I will."

Mr. Matthews said nothing, then lowered his fist and teetering slightly jerked Sarah along the corridor, shoving her out the front door—still in her leotard and tumbling shoes.

Coach James, lost in the moment, muttered, "That man is drunk and mean."

"What are we going to do?" Nick asked.

"I know what I'm going to do," the coach said. "First call the police, and then social services. The authorities finally need to know about this guy."

When Sarah didn't show up at practice the next day, Ally fretted: *She's in serious trouble.* The thought wouldn't leave, especially when Ally called Sarah's house that evening and no one answered.

On Friday Sarah arrived late at practice, hung her head, and wouldn't talk to anyone. Neither Ally nor Nick could make eye contact with her, and Ally could hardly wait to race to Sarah just before lunch. "What happened?" Ally put her hand on Sarah's arm.

"Nothing," Sarah said, pulling away. "Just leave me alone."

"Sarah, come on. What happened yesterday?"

"Nothing."

Ally studied Sarah's face. Sarah was wearing foundation—too much foundation—and blush. *But Sarah never wears makeup!*

"I can't talk to you," Sarah said, noticing Ally's stare. "You have to leave me alone."

John and Nick walked up where Sarah had been standing. "She has a bruise on her cheek," Nick whispered.

"Really?" Molly answered from behind.

"Let's not tell everyone," Ally whispered giving Molly the "I mean it" look, then gazed at the door Sarah had disappeared behind.

"We should tell the coach, though," Nick said. "He might be able to help, and he knows what's really going on."

As if on cue Coach James had just walked up. "I don't know everything or really anything," he said. "Social services normally sends a couple of people out to investigate—a social worker and a police officer. But if no one will press charges, there's not much anyone can do. It's a legal snafu." He stepped outside with Nick, Ally, and Molly right behind him.

"Making charges might just make it worse," Ally worried.

"But it's the only way out of that terrible circle of abuse," the coach said. "If only Sarah or her mother could understand that."

"I wonder what makes Mr. Matthews so mean," Molly said.

"He was in the military—maybe in Desert Storm," Nick suggested. "Maybe something awful happened and messed with his mind."

"Oh, come on," Ally challenged. "You've been watching too many movies."

"Mom was an Army brat," Nick insisted. "Her family moved every year, and her dad was tough, too. He was an officer during the first years of Vietnam before he retired. He told me a few times that the enlisted men often went through depression or became alcoholics because of what they had to go through in war."

"A lot of veterans certainly were wounded mentally," Coach James said, "but this is just speculation. Let's—"

"So Sarah's an Army brat?" Molly interrupted, wrinkling her nose with disgust. "That's not very nice, Nick."

"Just an expression, sister."

"Well, you may be a brat, but I'm not," Molly said.

"That's what you think."

"Let's not argue, kids," Coach James said. "And don't jump to conclusions. I'll find out what social services has done. Maybe they've at least started an investigation by now."

"But what if Sarah has to move away?" Molly said. "I've seen things like that on TV, where kids in unsafe situations are taken from their home or their parents move them. . . . Or . . . "

"Like I said," Coach James said, patting Molly's shoulder reassuringly, "let's not jump to conclusions." He wiped his forehead. "It's sure hot," he said, looking down the road that led to the Matthews's farm, and heading for his office. "Well, I'm going to make that call."

"I have a bad feeling," Molly said, suddenly getting Nick and Ally's attention. "Sarah told me once that her father and mother fought a lot. It scared her. I didn't want to pass it on because I felt she told me in confidence."

"When did she tell you this?" Nick said.

"At practice that second week. It seemed okay not to tell because her dad was being so nice about the honey and everything."

"I think there's reason to tell now," Ally said. "Of course, we can't report Mr. Matthews to the police. Only Sarah and her mother can do that. They have to bring charges if they're scared."

"But do you think Sarah's mother even knows how?" Nick said. He looked at Ally. "She's from Korea, right? They just moved to America—maybe she doesn't know about how things work here. Maybe she doesn't know the laws can protect you from even your own family."

"What are you saying?" Ally asked.

"I know her father let us sell the honey and all," Nick said. "But I get the feeling he's a volcano about to erupt. I sure don't want to see him rain down fire on Sarah or her mother."

John glanced at Ally and Molly furtively. "But I wouldn't want to be responsible for Sarah losing her father. Sarah loves him even if he is mean."

"Maybe we could just mail something without our names on it," Molly suggested. "Something only to Sarah's mother. To help. I bet my mom knows where we could get some information."

"What if Mr. Matthews intercepts it?" John asked. "He's probably the kind who opens everyone's mail even if it isn't for him. You know, an autocrat."

"A what?" Ally said.

"An autocrat," John said. "A dictator who rules with an iron hand. One person in charge of everyone. No one argues with him."

"Oh, that's what he is all right," Ally said, then turning to Molly, "I'm going to talk to my parents and see what they say. Maybe we should all do the same."

"Good idea," Nick said. "But I hope Coach James finds out something soon. Sarah can't go on like this."

As he and Molly started up the main road to their place, and John headed home too, Ally was left full of wonder and worry. *What if Sarah's father really has done something awful, and I have done nothing to try to prevent it?*

Eleven

Ally Learns to Trust

"No one knows what to do about Sarah," Ally told her parents that night at dinner.

"Mr. Matthews does sound like he is out of control," Mrs. O'Connor said, "but I think you'd better let Coach James handle it. You've already been in enough trouble with this man, and I don't want it going any farther."

"Neither do I," Ally said. "But Sarah's my friend!"

"What do you think, hon?" Mrs. O'Connor asked, looking at her husband.

"I think this is Mr. James's call. He saw what happened. Surely he understands the law. As the primary adult witness, I would leave it to him."

"We did think of sending Sarah's mom some information about abuse," Ally said. "Anonymously."

"That wouldn't be wise," Mr. O'Connor said. "Mr. Matthews might intercept the mail." He saw Ally frown.

Ally turned to her mother. "I guess it's best to let Coach James handle it."

"He's smart and cares about each of you," Mrs. O'Connor answered. "He wants Sarah to succeed, too, you know." She smiled at Ally. "You know it's always best, honey, to get the right people involved. That's what many government services are for—and pastors, and firemen. Don't try to be the hero when you may not know what you're doing."

"Okay," Ally said. "Mom, Dad, did you know Sarah practices gymnastics at home along with everything else she does? She said she'd show us her high bar, and we pictured a special piece of equipment. We thought it might be set up in her living room or den. Then she took us out to the tall oak tree right next to her house. Out from its trunk, about seven feet off the ground, was a bare limb almost parallel to the ground. Sarah had cleaned the bark off it herself, and it was worn smooth with her practice!"

"She sounds like a clever girl," Mrs. O'Connor said. "I think you've made a very nice friend—someone who will also be a friend to you, someone who gets things done when she has the opportunity to improve herself."

Mr. O'Connor squeezed Ally's arm.

"It thrills me," he said, "to see you care about someone in need. We saw it with the wild horses on the Outer Banks last summer too. You have a compassionate heart, Ally. Cultivate it. Never lose your tender spirit, and never be afraid of being sensitive and caring. But don't put yourself in harm's way."

"Don't try to be a hero, promise us?" Ally's mother added.

"What do you mean, Mom?"

"When you see someone mistreated, your natural inclination is to want to help. Not many people in our world lead the way in compassion and kindness. In fact, Christians are often the ones lagging behind."

"I don't think it's being a Christian that makes me want to help," Ally said. "I just want to—I care about Sarah. I don't necessarily think about being a Christian when I do it."

"It's the Spirit of God working in you," Mrs. O'Connor said. She walked over to the sink with a pile of dishes. "That's how God works in us. Subtly. He doesn't just tell us in his Word what to do. The Spirit actually speaks to our hearts with thoughts, impressions, suggestions, little ideas. I'm sure you don't realize it, but it's the Holy Spirit who puts the desire within you to help others."

"But I've seen others do that, and they're not even Christians."

"It's the Spirit of God working in them too, honey." Mrs. O'Connor smiled. "He works in all kinds of people at all levels. It's he who is ultimately behind all the good in the world. He guides people even when they don't know it. That's the beauty of the way God works. You never know whom he'll touch next. Just trust him to get the job done."

"I do."

"Good," she said, smiling, and walked back to sit down. "Ally, would you like some more dessert? There's one more piece of the walnut cake left."

"Sure!"

Mrs. O'Connor put the last piece of cake on a plate for Ally.

Ally's dad got up to flip on the coffeepot that was filled, ready, and waiting. "This little theory of yours," he asked his wife, "does that mean God is working in my boss, too—the terrible, very mean Mr. Roberts?"

"Sure is!"

"And how might that be, hon?"

"To keep him from being mean to you *all* the time."

Mr. O'Connor winked at Ally. "And since when were you a big theologian?"

Mrs. O'Connor smiled and sat back in her chair. "I think we should all pray about Sarah right now. We'll ask God to work. That poor girl has a tough row to hoe, and the the best thing any of us can do is pray, keep on loving her, and hope Mr. James is able to get social services in motion."

"I've been praying, Mom," Ally said, "and I'm not going to stop now."

"Then go ahead, honey."

Ally bowed her head. "Lord, please help Sarah and her dad and mom. Please keep Sarah safe in all the fighting, and if she needs help, then help her to come to us because we really do love her. Thanks for hearing me, Lord. Amen."

Ally's mom reached across the table and squeezed her daughter's hand. "You go, girl. Keep doing right. You'll never regret it."

"But I don't want to be some goody-goody, Mom."

"To be thoroughly good is not being a goody-goody, at least in the sense of a kid who never lets her humanity shine through. I don't mean that." Mrs. O'Connor paused to pour coffee for herself and her husband. "Jesus wants to make you like himself in character. That means strong as well as gentle. Truthful. Loving, even when it's tough."

"Sometimes I think," Ally said, "I'll never be like him."

Ally's father grabbed the coffee cream from the fridge and set it on the table. "We see Jesus working in you, honey," he said. "All the time. You're making an impact."

"I am?" Ally took a big bite of the delicious cake. The creamy icing tasted so good she wished it would never end.

"Sure. Molly, John, and even Nick look up to you. You're never more like Jesus than when you just live right without thinking about being like Jesus."

"I guess."

"No need to guess," Mrs. O'Connor said. "God gives us that assurance." She leaned down and whispered into Ally's ear, "We just want you to know we're proud of you."

Ally felt embarrassed for a moment, but it was a good embarrassment. Her dad got up to wash the dishes, while

Ally finished the cake in another minute and lingered outside. She had a lot to think about: *God is working in Sarah's life, but right now it isn't obvious at all.*

"I trust you, God," she prayed without thinking about it. "I trust you to help Sarah whether I see it or not."

Sarah Opens Her Heart

At the gym on Monday morning, Ally waited for Sarah, then wasted no time in asking how things were going at home. She only hoped Sarah would be open and honest.

"Well, two people from the state visited on Saturday," Sarah told her. "They told my father if there were more reports of mistreatment, they'd do a major investigation. He was really mad." Then Sarah brightened. "But he was quiet all weekend. He didn't yell at me or my mother for three days, and he said I could come back to practice."

"So you're going to be able to go to the competition?" Ally asked.

"Well," Sarah said, "if Dad doesn't start drinking it might be . . . " She paused.

"I know your dad gets angry when he drinks," Ally whispered. "I've seen it, smelled the alcohol on his breath. You don't have to hide from me, Sarah."

She looked relieved. "It's not really any secret here any-more, is it?" she sighed. "Anyway, Dad knows that doing my chores is not a problem. I always do them. He just gets confused, I think, when he drinks too much."

"Do you think your father is scared now?" Nick asked, overhearing enough to know he could ask outright.

"I don't know," Sarah said. "But that's not necesssar-ily good because when he's scared, sometimes he drinks even more. My mother seems relieved since those peo-ple visited, so something must be better somehow."

"Practice time," Coach James called, clapping his hands.

❧

"Coach James, did you hear what happened at Sarah's house?" Ally asked after practice, when the other team-mates had already drifted outside.

"Yes," the coach nodded. "She told me this morning. I'm glad the state acted quickly. Maybe this will make Mr. Matthews think twice before he comes in here rough, incoherent, and reeking of alcohol."

"We're praying that Sarah and her father will work out their problems," Ally said, gesturing toward Nick, John, Molly, and Sarah at the other end of the gym.

Coach James smiled. "It's not Sarah's problem to work out, Ally. It's her father's. Remember that. He needs to learn to control his drinking and his temper. By the way, are you walking Sarah home today?"

Ally nodded.

"Then you'd better get going so she's not delayed get-ting back."

Ally nodded and caught up to Sarah, Nick, John, and Molly on their way into the corridor. Molly was standing with her arm around Sarah's shoulder like a best buddy.

Sarah was telling them, "I never wanted to say any-thing. I'm ashamed of my dad. I've wished, . . . well, you all have such nice dads. I've wanted mine to be like that too. Sometimes I'm afraid to go home to find out what he's done to my mom. I'm afraid of what he might do to me, too, even when I've done everything he's asked. I'm used to being slapped, but I'm still afraid," she confessed.

"You can call on us, Sarah, anytime," Nick said. "You don't have to ever be scared—or slapped. That doesn't have to happen. It shouldn't happen."

"I'm beginning to trust you guys," Sarah said, wiping a tear. "I've wanted to tell you what it's really like—it's so different to be able to talk to you. I've never been able to do this before now."

"It's okay," Molly reassured. "It's going to be okay."

They walked along in silence until they reached Sarah's road. They could see Mr. Matthews on the tractor in the far cornfield, trimming the corn. Then Sarah's mother stepped out of the house and offered everyone Kool-Aid.

"You want Coke, too?" Mrs. Matthews said, her eyes hopeful for the first time, instead of afraid and ashamed. Ally could tell she was glad for their friendship.

"Thanks, the Kool-Aid is great," Ally said.

"You want to see some of my mom's sewing?" Sarah asked. She led them into a room festooned with colorful samplers, cross-stitched table covers, and an exotic bedspread embroidered with strutting peacocks.

"Mom thinks she might try and sell some of these," Sarah said, putting her arm through her mother's. "She's an expert at it."

"My great-grandmother teach me," Mrs. Matthews said. There was a glow of happiness in her face that Ally had never seen before.

❧

Suddenly Mr. Matthews stomped into the sewing room. Ally could see the panic on Sarah's face. It was clear: Sarah feared her father.

But with calmness Sarah began to talk as if everything was fine. "Dad," she said, "I wish sometime you would let me show my friends what a great horse Colonel is."

"Just don't wear him out," her father answered just as calmly.

Sarah seemed shocked at his consent, so much that she fumbled for what to say. "Yes, . . . sure, . . . yes, Dad."

When Mr. Matthews disappeared into the back of the house, Sarah started smiling from ear to ear. "I never expected him to let me take you for a ride," she said, heading for the kitchen. Ally, Nick, Molly, and John followed, depositing their Kool-Aid glasses by the sink. "C'mon," Sarah said, "let's go for a ride!" She rushed to the barn, everyone in tow.

"First, I should clean out Colonel's stall," Sarah said.

Nick picked up the pitchfork to help. "You go ahead and saddle Colonel," he said. "I'll work the pooper scooper."

Molly rolled her eyes. "You just wanted to say that," she quipped.

"Why is your father so nice about the horse today?" Ally asked as Sarah picked up the saddle.

"Anything that's good for the horse is good enough for Dad," Sarah said.

"You'd think he cares more for Colonel than your family," Ally said. Sarah stopped a second, and Ally added, "Well, he's different when he talks about Colonel."

"I know," Sarah admitted, but kept silent. She finished saddling Colonel, then led him into the sunlit corral. "You sit behind me, Ally. I don't think my dad would let you ride him alone."

"Okay!" Ally said.

Sarah mounted the horse, then held out her hand to pull up Ally. Colonel trotted out of the yard, excited for what promised to be a brisk ride. When they reached the drive-way, Sarah clucked and gently kicked his side. Colonel boomed into a full canter down the road.

"Hold on!" Sarah yelled.

Wind whipped at her auburn hair, but Ally held on, relishing the moment. They cantered around to the main gate, then Sarah slowed Colonel for the turn onto the path by the cornfield. Once again, Sarah nudged Colonel into a canter. The rocking-chair motion of the gait was wonderful. Ally whooped along with Sarah.

"Should I put him into full tilt?" Sarah asked over her shoulder.

"Go for it!" Ally cried.

"Hold on!"

Sarah kicked hard, and suddenly Colonel bolted into the smooth, wild gait of the gallop. Hooves pounded. The air swirled. The smell of corn and dust filled Ally's nostrils. They rode around the cornfield, up to the pond, then back to the barnyard. Sarah slowed down to a bouncy trot as they passed Mr. Matthews working on his tractor.

Afterward, Sarah took Molly, Nick, and John, in turn, for rides. "This was one of my best days," she said an hour later when everyone started for home.

"There'll be many more," Ally said, Nick, Molly, and John nodding in agreement.

At gymnastics practice the next day Sarah seemed so much more relaxed. She even helped Nick, coming back from his time-out to mend, get down his handspring. Ally was still working on her vault routine, but not making much progress—and the first competitive meet was one week away! This was the week to prepare expectantly, Coach James urged. "Remember, we can face giants," Nick said later.

Giants there were, Ally learned the next day—but not necessarily in the gym. Sarah told Ally that the social worker had stopped by the day before. The woman, Sarah said, was stern-faced with careful, watchful eyes and a no-nonsense attitude. She wasn't particularly friendly, which Sarah said made her dad nervous. He'd paced the floor, answering her questions with short, cut-and-dried answers.

"My dad doesn't like her," Sarah said. She had that worried look again. "My mom and I kept quiet about him hitting us. I just can't talk about it right now. I don't want to hurt my dad."

"But how will you get help if you don't talk?" Nick said, coming up on the conversation.

"We'll work it out," Sarah said, smiling wanly. "I just can't snitch on my dad."

Nick and Ally insisted on walking Sarah home that afternoon.

"Good," Nick said when they arrived at the farm. He'd noticed Mr. Matthews's truck was gone. No explanation was needed on what Nick was thinking—but the missing pickup wasn't necessarily good.

"I hope he's not drinking," Sarah said, as she led everyone into the house.

Everything was quiet, though, while Sarah led her friends in a few quick games of Crazy Eights while they drank Kool-Aid and ate popcorn.

Maybe things are going to be okay, Ally thought as she talked everyone into meeting later that evening at the clubhouse for a camp-out. Sarah's mother gave her permission; everyone called their parents to settle things. The camp-out was on, and, in fact, Ally's parents would invite the other moms and dads to go out for dinner too.

❧

At dusk Nick and Molly hauled their Monopoly game board and flashlights to the clubhouse, with Ally and John right behind carrying the submarine sandwiches, chips, and cookies Mrs. O'Connor made for their camp-out.

"It doesn't get better than this," Nick said, digging into the chips as Ally and Molly cracked open the Monopoly board.

"It will be better," Ally said, "when Sarah gets here." Everyone nodded and went ahead to a game of Monopoly by flashlight. They had just started in on the sandwiches when Ally heard a cry from the woods. She shone a flashlight into the trees. Sarah was whimpering and running toward them!

"Dad's gone crazy," she cried. "He's out of control. Please, help!"

Her lower lip was cut and bleeding, and her right cheek was red, already bruising from a blow. Ally reached out to touch Sarah's face, but Sarah grabbed her arm and pulled. He's beating Mom," she cried. "We've got to do something."

"Run! Call 9–1–1!" Ally told Molly. "Come on, Nick, you and John, come on."

"No, please," Sarah said. "That's what my dad's mad about—he's mad about the social worker intruding on our life. He told me if I called the police again, he'd kill Mom. Just help me get my mother away!"

Ally felt confused. If the police had already been there at the Matthews's house, what good was it to call them again?

Sarah wailed, "Come, please just come and help me talk to him. Then we can get my mother away."

"Has your father been drinking?" Nick asked. It seemed to him that Sarah still wasn't making the connection between her father's drinking and his meanness; she wasn't seeing he was out of control by something beyond his power. "Will your mother press charges to get him some help and keep him away when he's drunk?"

"Nick, she won't turn against him," Sarah cried, "and I have to obey my mother."

"It doesn't have to be like this," Nick insisted. "You can get help—the police can get you all help."

Ally realized Nick was right, but time was running out. They had to take action—with or without the police. They had to get to Mrs. Matthews now.

"Molly, you and John stay here to tell our parents where we are when they get home," Ally said. "Nick and I will go together over to the Matthews's." Molly and John nodded as Ally continued, "We can take my dad's mobile phone from his car, since he and Mom went in the Parkers' car. Then if we have to, we can call the police. All right, let's go." She raced up the path to Sarah's, Nick and Sarah behind her, praying as she raced.

But it was Sarah's prayer, voiced between gasps for air and the soft pounding of their feet on the soil, that almost stopped Ally.

"Please, God," Sarah said chokingly as they ran, "these friends have helped me so much . . . save my mom, help my dad see the truth . . . I know you can help him."

Ally called back, "Pray, and keep praying!"

The night air was cool and brisk. It seemed so peaceful. *How can such bad things be happening so close to home on a night like this?* Ally wondered as her heart thumped wildly in her chest.

The Terrible Night

"Remember, he's my dad," Sarah said as they neared her house. "He's still my dad, even if he is mean when he drinks too much."

"We're not going to forget that," Nick said.

Ally's knees were shaking. She imagined what might happen if Mr. Matthews had a gun or something.

"All we're doing is getting your mother out of there," Nick said, "till your Dad can sober up, right?"

"I guess that's a good plan," Sarah said, interrupted by shouting and the sound of china breaking against a wall.

"He's really going at it," Nick said, looking apprehensive for the first time. He turned off his flashlight as they crept below the kitchen windows. Ally peered in to see Mrs. Matthews cowering in the corner, her dress ripped and her hands to her face. Mr. Matthews stood on the other side of the room with a stack of plates in his hand.

"You want me to drop this—is that what you want?" he shouted. "You want me to destroy everything?"

"I not call social worker!" Sarah's mom yelled back. "I know nothing of it."

"I know you—always protecting Sarah! It was you!"

"It wasn't!"

"Tell the truth!"

Mr. Matthews held a plate out, then flicked it so it sailed into the cabinets. It shattered, sending pieces every which way. Mrs. Matthews screamed, "Stop!" but he threw another, this one crashing into the sink.

"You ruin us all!" Mrs. Matthews shouted.

"I don't care!" Mr. Matthews yelled back.

Ally whispered to Nick and Sarah, "What do we do? He's sick—gone crazy!"

Nick sucked his lip. He looked in the window another time. That's it," he told Sarah. "Call the police."

Sarah shook her head no.

"But we can't stop him," Nick said.

Ally agreed. "You saw what he did to Coach James that day. What would he do to us?"

A plate shattered inside the house. Mrs. Matthews screamed again, and everyone jumped.

"Use the phone," Nick said. "Do it!"

Ally took out the hand-held flip phone and punched 9–1–1. A female dispatcher came on and Ally said, "We need help at the Matthews's farm!" She turned to Sarah. "What's the address here?"

"120 Carleton Road."

Sarah grabbed the phone from Ally.

"Didn't we just have some officers out there?" the dispatcher asked.

"Yes," she said, "but the situation is worse. My father is throwing dishes at my mother. He's going to hurt her."

"We'll have a patrol car there. You kids stay outside—"

Nick grabbed the phone from Sarah, clicking it off. "He heard us!" Nick said, his voice quavering. "Run!"

The front door slammed open. "What are you doing here?" Mr. Matthews bellowed. "You stay there," he shouted after Ally and Nick who were sprinting toward the barn.

Ally pulled Nick to a stop about a hundred yards from the house. "Where's Sarah?" she panted. "Sarah's not with us." She could hear Nick panting in the darkness of the trees, but couldn't see his face or anything beyond. A cloud had just moved over the moon.

"Let's go over the dam and come in the back of the house," Nick said. "He's probably going to start hitting Sarah. We have to get inside."

"What about the police?"

"We'll be able to see them when they come up the road."

"What do you think he'll say?"

"That nothing's wrong."

"Then what do we do?"

"We tell the cops what we saw."

"C'mon, we've got to hurry."

Ally whisked over the dam before Nick. They could hear water splashing down the little waterfall with a rushing sound. Moonlight burned through the drifting night clouds, but not in time for Nick to see the muck at the edge of the pond. His shoe squished down into it with a sucking noise.

"So much for my Adidas," he muttered, running after Ally through the trees.

In the moonlight Ally traipsed by one of the beehives. *No buzzing*, Ally thought. *The bees must be asleep in the hives.* She pulled her sweatshirt close, wondering if Nick was as scared as she was. She didn't want to get stung at this hour—and she didn't want anyone to get hurt at the Matthews's house.

Fifty feet from the house, Nick and Ally stopped for a minute in the trees. An undergrowth of brambles, rose bushes, and other vegetation protected the back door from their reach.

"We've got to hurry," Ally whispered, motioning to a side door.

As they threaded their way through the undergrowth, headlights cut through the thicket. They heard a car crunch to a stop in the yard.

"The police!" Nick said.

"We've got to get in there!" Ally nodded toward the house. "What if Mr. Matthews convinces Sarah and her mom to say everything's okay?"

Nick pushed through the underbrush.

"Rats!" he cried, coming to a dead end in the path. "We'll never get there in time."

"Let's call them and tell them to wait," Ally said. She took out the phone and pushed the on switch.

Nothing happened.

Ally pushed it again.

"It's dead!"

"Dead?" Nick said. "How?"

"I must have left it on. Dad plugs it into the car cigarette lighter. But he may not have charged it recently."

"What are we going to do now? We have to tell the police what's happening, because you can be sure Mr. Matthews won't. If he heard us calling before, he might have cleaned up the kitchen and all the evidence."

Ally nodded. "Hurry."

They backtracked through the underbrush, looking for another trail back to the house. They finally had to circle around, almost to the edge of the next farm. When they did reach the Matthews's yard, there wasn't a police car in sight.

"They came and left," Nick said with anger. "We were too late."

"Look," Ally said. Above them a window stood half open on the second floor.

"Give me a boost," Nick said. "I'm going in."

"What about me?"

"Go around to the front. Maybe we can make a diversion."

Ally made a step-up for Nick with her fingers linked together. Nick set his right foot in and grabbed the ledge of the window with his fingertips. Ally hoisted him upward. A second later he heaved his body over the ledge and disappeared inside. Then he leaned out and whispered, "I'm in a bedroom. I'll try to find a phone. If you can, sneak in the front door."

Ally crept along the edge of the house to the front door. Only the screen door was shut and she could hear shouting from inside.

"You called the police again!" Mr. Matthews roared. "You're going to pay for this."

Ally couldn't stand it. She reached for the door handle. Mr. Matthews was shouting with his back to her, but staggering toward Sarah and her mother, huddled in front of the kitchen sink. Sarah started shrieking, her mom sobbing as Mr. Matthews leered toward them. Ally pulled the door noiselessly toward herself, spotting Nick in the shadows of the next room. He was mouthing something. *What was he saying?*

"Shout something!" Nick mouthed.

Ally frowned in confusion.

"Shout. Something," Nick mouthed again.

Praying that Mr. Matthews wouldn't kick her out the door with one foot, she shouted, "Look out!"

Mr. Matthews spun around as Nick bolted from the shadows into the kitchen. He started to slam into Mr. Matthews, but lost his balance, crashing through the front door and tripping over Ally. Sprawled out on the front porch, Nick rolled to get up. Ally leaped to the side as Mr. Matthews bolted after Nick, running toward the nearby rows of corn.

Ally ran through the front door, locking it behind her.

"Where's your phone?" she yelled to Sarah.

"It doesn't work," Sarah said.

"We cannot pay our bill," Mrs. Matthews cried. Sarah's eyes widened with fright as she waved to the wall again, then cried, "Oh no!"

At that moment, the door thumped. Mr. Matthews was ramming it with something. "Let me in!" he yelled, muffled only by the door between them.

Suddenly a voice called from upstairs. Nick had circled around and climbed back in the second-story window by way of the tree. "Come on," he shouted.

"Let me in!" the voice bellowed again.

Sarah looked at Ally. "He's going to break down that door," she cried.

Nick motioned with his hands. "Up the stairs!" he whispered.

The front door shivered as Mr. Matthews blasted into it one more time. This time the latch jumped in position, but it didn't break. Nick ran downstairs by himself and held it down. "I hope this door doesn't buckle."

"My dad has broken it before," Sarah cried as she climbed the stairs. "To the attic!"

Behind them, the door crashed again. This time it splintered and began to buckle.

"We don't have much time," Nick said. "Hurry."

Up the stairs, Ally pulled the phone out of her pocket. It was still dead.

Nick ran to a window and said, "Maybe we could jump."

"No, no!" Mrs. Matthews sobbed.

"Okay," Nick said. "It's okay. Our strength is in outsmarting him."

Our strength can only be in you, Ally prayed silently. *God, help us.* She pulled shut the door to the attic as suddenly the whole house seemed to shatter. The front door of the house had given way. Mr. Matthews was back in the house.

Fourteen

Attic Escape

Dust bunnies, stacked furniture, racks of clothing, and boxes of junk made the attic a confusing maze. Still, Sarah and her mother managed to hide behind one of the racks. Nick positioned a chair under the doorknob to keep it from opening, while Ally braced other chairs behind it.

"What do we do now?" Ally asked.

"Wait for him to give up or fall into a drunken stupor," Nick said. "Then we try to escape."

"What if he gets into the attic? We'd be cornered three stories up. There's no way out."

There was a sudden bang on the door.

"You! In there!" Mr. Matthews shouted.

"He found us quick!" Nick said.

Everyone watched the door strain on its hinges from the impact of Mr. Matthews hitting it. "You don't open up, I'm going to smoke you out!" he shouted.

"Smoke us?" Nick said.

"What does he mean?" Ally asked.

At that moment the lights went out.

"He must have gone down to the breaker box," Nick said, fumbling for his pocket flashlight." Nick shone a thin beam of light across the chairs piled in front of the door. Nothing looked amiss.

"We've got to go for help," Nick said. "We have to—no one knows we're here."

"I wish this phone worked," Ally said, taking the handset out one more time and checking it.

Mr. Matthews banged against the door again. Everyone shuddered. The huge man's voice rang loud and clear. "You don't open up, I'm gonna smoke ya out, you hear me?"

"Just stay away from us!" Nick shouted.

There was silence one more time. Then Ally noticed something dark fluttering in through a vent in the door.

Nick shone the flashlight on it.

"Smoke! He must have got his beehive smoker from the barn."

Mrs. Matthews coughed and shivered with fright. The thick smoke quickly rose, filling the attic with a thick, acrid, nasty smell. *No wonder it knocks out bees,* Ally thought. She motioned to everyone in the light of Nick's flashlight to cover their mouths. Sarah grabbed towels off one of the piles of clothing and passed them around. Still the smoke stung everyone's eyes and lungs. Ally felt as if she couldn't breathe. She knew that smoke inhalation was a main way people die in fires. *We have to get out of the attic, but how?*

Nick must have been thinking the same thing as he began to try and open one of the windows.

Sarah choked, "There's another way." She pointed to the chimney stack at the other end of the attic. Its bricks were exposed, and from its left side iron bars—steps in a ladder—protruded. Ally looked up and saw a little hatch at the top of the ladder, next to the chimney.

100

"It's for getting onto the roof," Sarah said between coughs. "The roof is flat and has an observation area. The people who built it liked to look at the stars from up there. See, there's an old telescope in that box right there." She pointed to a large scope mounted on a rickety tripod.

Nick thought the route to the roof might be just the way out they needed. "Maybe we could grab tree branches from the roof and shimmy down."

"Are you kidding?" Ally grabbed Nick's shoulder.

Sarah turned to her mother. "Mom, can you climb down the tree?"

"I can get to roof," Mrs. Matthews said.

"I'd better go first," Sarah said. "I've been there before." She climbed the ladder, opened the latch, then thrust upward. The hatch squeaked open. In a moment she had slipped through. Nick pointed the flashlight upward, and Sarah blinked back from on top of the hatch hole. Smoke billowed up. "Come on," she said between coughs. "Hurry."

Ally helped Mrs. Matthews, who climbed agilely. In a few seconds, she reached the top and pushed through. The smoke was so thick now that Ally could barely see. Nick was hacking and choking below.

Ally climbed a bar at a time, moving as quickly as she could. A moment later she stood on the roof, drawing in the first clean breaths of air she'd had in minutes.

Nick followed, gasping. "Fresh air," he said, throwing down his towel. "Come on, we have to move before he figures out what we've done."

"I stay here," Mrs. Matthews said.

Sarah grasped her mother's hands. "Ally, go. Get some help. The next farm!"

Nick looked at Ally. "Do you think you can do this?" Ally nodded, and Nick turned.

"Sarah, you've got to go, too. All of us. Leap for a branch. We can't wait."

"I'll stay with my mother," Sarah said. "I have to."

"But your father won't find us," Ally said, "if we go now." She moved to the edge of the roof and peered down. It looked like miles to the ground. But the tree branches extended close to the top of the roof. *We could leap and grab hold of one of the thickest branches even though it would be risky. Can we find a sturdy branch to grab hold of without falling first? Will the branches crack under our weight and break?* Ally shivered.

"I'll go first," Nick said.

"No, I will," Ally said. "You wait till the last minute in case Mr. Matthews gets up on the roof."

"Be careful," he said, shining the light on the branches.

The roof was encircled by a foot-high brick wall. Ally stood on the little wall, her heart jolting in her chest. Smoke poured out the hatch hole in the roof. She gave one last look back. "Here goes," she whispered as she leapt into the tree, clutching for anything to anchor her weight.

Her hands clasped a thick branch jutting out toward the house. Ally swung lightly, then set her feet on a lower branch. She climbed down and leaped quickly to the ground. *Coach James would be proud,* she thought.

"It's easy," she called, relieved.

Nick pointed the flashlight. "Go ahead, Sarah. You're next."

"I'll stay with my mother."

"Okay. Here's the flash." He handed her the flashlight, then leaped and grabbed the same branch Ally had. It creaked from his pull and started to crack. Nick quickly sank to a lower branch and found his way to the ground.

Just then Ally saw the window open slowly.

"I'm gon-na get you!" Mr. Matthews slurred.

Nick hit the ground and he and Ally sprinted toward the neighbors, Mr. Matthews shouting after them. "You won't escape this time!"

"To the dam," Nick hollered at Ally. He stopped to pick up a stone, hurling it back at Mr. Matthews as they ran.

Moments later their feet slapped down on the edge of the dam. Ally picked up some stones to fling at Mr. Matthews, too, but the big man was sober enough to dodge out of the way.

Breathless, Nick said, "I've got an idea."

He wiped mud on his face and hands. "Hey!" he yelled. "Betcha can't catch me!" He waved his arms, then screeched, "I'm gonna go ride Colonel!"

Nick darted off toward the barn with Mr. Matthews after him and Ally not far behind. Nick circled the barn, and Mr. Matthews stumbled long enough for Nick to catch up with Ally hiding at the edge of the yard.

"Come with me," Nick called. They ran down to the orchard where the beehives were kept. "Run straight through," Nick shouted. "Run right by all the hives."

"What are you going to do?" Ally gasped.

"Just run!" Nick said. "If anything happens, follow the trail and get to the next farm up for help. Call 9–1–1. That's our best hope."

Mr. Matthews came around the edge of the barn. With a rumble, he tore off after them.

"Go!" Nick shouted. "Now."

Ally sprinted right by the beehives. There were no bees in sight. Upon reaching the other side of the orchard, Ally turned around to see Nick opening the hives. Bees burned through the air in anger. *What?* Ally thought.

Then she got it: *Nick had caked on the mud to protect himself.* She saw Mr. Matthews lunge at Nick, then halt.

"Oww. Oww!" Mr. Matthews yelped. He swore and cried in pain, then crumpled to the ground.

Ally ran up the trail toward the next house. But something in the air made her stop. She turned. There against the darkness, flames were leaping into the air at the Matthews's house.

"Sarah!" Ally cried, her feet instinctively breaking forward.

Fifteen

The Leap for Life

Ally sprinted across the farmland toward the burning house.

"Sarah!" she screamed.

Praying for all she was worth, Ally reached the road. The dogs swirled out around her. As she ran up the road toward the house she could see Sarah and her mother on the rooftop platform. Mrs. Matthews held her hands up to her face to shield herself from the heat. From the lower windows, tendrils of flame licked up the sides of the house. Smoke jetted from all the other windows and blotted out the stars.

"Sarah!" Ally called from the base of the tree. "Look at me. We've got to get you down!"

But Ally's voice couldn't be heard. Sirens screamed in the distance.

Within moments Nick joined Ally to stare helplessly skyward. The fire roared through the house like a hurricane, a deafening noise.

104

Ally got as close to the house as she dared and yelled, "Sarah, jump to the tree! The tree, Sarah! The tree!"

"They can't hear you," Nick shouted above the roar. Mrs. Matthews leaned backwards over the edge, as if trying to get away from the flames. Sarah appeared to be pleading with her mother.

Suddenly, as sirens shrieked, a fire truck careened into the yard, then turned around and went back out.

"They're looking for a fireplug!" Nick shouted.

"Come on," Ally said. "Let's get the fireman."

"Maybe they have a life net," Nick said. "You know, a kind of trampoline that people can jump into." He hurried off. "We need the life net," he shouted to one fireman. Nick motioned to the roof.

The fireman ran back to the truck, opened a side door, and pulled out a huge collapsible net. Within seconds his crew helped him yank it open up to full size, about ten feet across, a bulls eye painted in the middle of the white canvas. Six firemen hauled the net to the edge of the house.

"Jump!" one of the men called up to Sarah and her mother, "and try to land on your back or your rear end."

Sarah shook her head in confusion. Another fireman pulled out a bullhorn. "You have to jump. The fire is out of control. You have to jump now."

Mrs. Matthews stood on the little ledge covering her face with her hands.

Ally tugged the fireman's arm. "They're afraid," she cried. "But they'll listen to me, I think. Let me talk to them."

The fireman showed her what button to push and Ally pointed the horn toward Sarah. "Sarah, jump with your mother. It's the only way. Into the life net. Now. Right now!"

"No jumping!" Mrs. Matthews cried.

"She's too afraid," Sarah shouted.

"It's the only way," Ally shouted again through the bullhorn.

Mrs. Matthews pulled her hands from her face. She grabbed Sarah's hand. Sarah's face was twisted with fear, and her mother was trembling. *It's Sarah who's afraid to jump*, Ally realized. "Please, Lord," she prayed silently. "Help us." She shut her eyes for just a second, and blinking them open saw Mrs. Matthews grab Sarah about the waist and then leaned back, plummeting with Sarah in her arms onto the life net. They hit, bouncing, but still holding onto each other, a ball of tangled legs and arms.

The firemen laid down the net, helped them off, and carried them from the house which was about to explode in flames. They ran, rounding the barnyard just as a sickening boom and blast of heat spewed toward them.

Sarah's eyes went wide. "The barn! Colonel!"

Sarah pulled away from the fireman's grasp and darted for the barn. From behind Mr. Matthews had limped into the barnyard, bitten mercilessly by the bees all over his face and limbs. Oblivious to the pain, he turned toward the barn and shouted: "Colonel!"

Firemen held Mrs. Matthews, Nick, and Ally a safe distance away and began to douse the fire. A second truck careened into the drive as Sarah and her father turned into the burning barn. Colonel was rearing and kicking in his stall.

"We have to get him out," Sarah yelled.

She opened the gate as Mr. Matthews whistled. Colonel darted out, then seeing the flames, ran back.

Mr. Matthews staggered and tried to force Colonel forward, but the horse's eyes blinked with terror. His ears laid back on his head.

"Cover his eyes," Sarah yelled. "I saw it once in a movie."

Mr. Matthews took off his shirt. Bee stings covered his upper torso. Sarah had never seen anyone so badly scarred with welts from the honeybees. The big man pulled the shirt over Colonel's eyes and tied it by the sleeves under his neck.

Just as he did so, the barn caught fire.

106

"Run," Sarah yelled. "Run!"

Mr. Matthews led the horse on one side—Sarah on the other—directly past the flames and through the large doors and outside. Mr. Matthews pulled his shirt from Colonel's face as they joined Nick, Ally, and Mrs. Matthews huddled in the road. Firemen continued to battle the flames, as Mr. Matthews sank to his haunches. He looked up at Nick and Ally. His voice choked as he mumbled, "You saved my family."

Before Ally or Nick could say a word, a police car screeched into the yard. Mr. Matthews let go of Colonel and held up his hands. "I guess you're here for me," he told the driver.

The police led Mr. Matthews to the back of their car as Sarah squeezed Ally's hand. Tears were pouring down her face.

"You're okay now," Ally said, "your mom is okay, and your dad is going to get help. He's not going to be able to hurt you anymore. We're all safe."

Sarah buried her head in Ally's hair.

"Your dad will get help now," Nick repeated. "If he can change, he can come back and take care of you."

Sarah's mother was shivering with fear while a police officer questioned her. Ally heard her say, "Yes, I hope. But now I know I can't change him. Only he can change himself."

"Maybe with God's help . . . " Ally added, speaking to no one in particular.

"With God's help," Sarah said as she looked up, unembarrassed by her red, tear-stained face.

Nick fidgeted and looked helpless, surrounded by three brave but tearful women. He tried to make a joke to offset the emotion of the moment.

"Ah Nick," Ally said, giving him a playful whap on the back of the head. "Maybe you ought to just stick to fighting giants."

Sixteen

The Big Finish

Since Sarah and her mother had gone to stay with relatives in another state, no one expected the first gymnastics competition to go well. Everyone was still murmuring about the fire at the Matthews's farm, but Coach James kept them focused on all the routine-polishing left to do.

"I know you're all upset Sarah's not here," Coach James said, gathering the team around him at a break. "But you all know about the tragedy that struck her family last weekend. I know if she could be here, she would." He gave everyone a few pointers for Friday, their last practice before the competition.

Everyone practiced hard the next day, but few team members could do any of the major tumbles and no one performed a solid handspring. Coach James gathered everyone for one last pep talk. Clearly, he was discouraged as he stood before the small group, but he was trying to boost

spirits—let everyone know it was their personal perform-
ance he cared about, not just winning.

"You know, you've worked hard," he told them. "Tomorrow is your first chance at competition. You're not going
to score many points at first. But if you keep trying and
keep hanging in there no matter how you feel, it'll pay off."

Ally thought about her prayers for Sarah and about how
discouraged she had felt. Her parents had encouraged her
to keep believing God would work things out. Like the
coach was saying, she had learned it was important to hang
in there and keep trying.

The creak of the door interrupted her thoughts. *Sarah!*
Ally smiled! Sarah emerged with her mother.

"Sarah!" the team cried.

Coach James spun around as everyone leapt to their
feet, smiling, cheering, and crowding around Sarah.

"We thought you weren't going to be here."

"We've missed you!"

"No—worse! We stink without you."

"My mom and I are coming back here to town," Sarah
said, smiling. "She got one job as a cook and another as a
seamstress, so I'm going to go to school here this fall."

Everyone cheered.

Sarah grabbed Ally and Nick and gave them each a light
kiss on the cheek. "I love you guys," she said. Nick blushed,
but Sarah didn't see it. She'd turned to hug Molly, John,
and finally Coach James.

"You all helped me realize it wasn't my fault that I was
being hurt," she told everyone. "You showed me that it's
better to get help than to keep thinking things will change
by themselves. Now my dad is going to counseling while
he's in jail, and we get to visit him every week. He's sorry,
and he's going to join a group for alcoholics. He says he's
really going to try to change."

Coach James nodded and gave Sarah a long hug.

"Okay," Sarah finally said, wiping away tears, "I'm ready. What are we doing first—tumbling, balance beam, or uneven bars?"

It was now as if Sarah had never been gone, only everyone began to practice their events with more energy and enthusiasm than ever. Ally overheard Coach James say, "I think we have a chance to place, but even if we don't, we'll have the best team spirit at the meet!"

Ally marveled as Sarah performed: *Thanks, Lord. This is excellent. Excellent!* "Thank you, God!" she prayed right out loud. Then remembering her own flying leap to the tree from the Matthews's rooftop, Ally burst forward and flew onto the vault. At that moment, she knew that with God's help there was nothing she—or anyone else—could not do.

How to Detect Abuse*

Abuse occurs in many forms, whether it's physical, sexual, or emotional, but no type of abuse should be tolerated. What can you do if you suspect someone is being abused? First, look for these warning signals (especially a combination of these signals):

- Constant depression
- Refusal to communicate
- Acting out in terms of making threats or unnecessarily disobeying codes of conduct or accepted behavior
- Threats of violence or suicide
- Attempts at suicide
- A sullen, angry disposition
- A sudden drop in grades or class participation
- Mood swings, from great happiness to great depression
- Constant talk of wanting to get away from home or away from someone
- Running away
- A sense of isolation, believing that no one cares
- Drug or alcohol abuse
- Sexual promiscuity
- Sudden change in musical tastes to much more violent music (heavy metal, punk, grunge)

Like Ally and her friends did with Sarah, try talking with your friend. See if he or she will open up and be candid about the situation. You may be rebuffed or told nothing is wrong, but listen to your conscience. If you see signs of abuse, persevere to try to get at the truth.

Sometimes suspected abuse might be nothing more than the mood swings of a typical teenager. If the signs persist, however, talk to an adult to see if a meeting can be arranged with your friend. Consider doing an "intervention," in which a number of people—friends, pastors, people in authority—sit down with your friend and try to help him or her.

Stay in communication with the person you suspect is being abused. Consider offering a place of refuge in your home if your parents will consider it—and involve a counselor or social worker. Most importantly, remain a true friend. Pray for the person, show acts of kindness, and offer encouragement. The recovery period for abuse is long, and a solid friendship will help in the healing process. The love of many individuals—starting with you—can help.

*Some of this information is taken from Jay Kesler's *Family Forum*, (Colorado Springs: Victor Books, 1984).

Mark Littleton, a former pastor and youth pastor, is a writer and a speaker at churches, retreats, conferences, and other Christian gatherings. He is happily married to Jeanette Gardner and has three children, Nicole, Alisha, and Gardner, also known as Gard-zilla the Destroyer because, at three years old, he is able to destroy whole cities when left unattended for more than thirty seconds. Mark and his family have a dog named Patches and a cat named Beauty, who is afraid of the dog. Mark collects lighthouses, original paintings of ships, and hundred dollar bills. He is willing to add any contributions you might wish to make to his collections, especially the hundred dollar bill collection.